PETITE FLEUR

PETITE FLEUR

Iosi Havilio

Translated by Lorna Scott Fox

SHEFFIELD – LONDON – NEW HAVEN

First published in the UK by And Other Stories
Sheffield – London – New Haven
www.andotherstories.org

Originally published as *Pequeña Flor*
© 2015 Iosi Havilio
Translation © 2017 Lorna Scott Fox

9 8 7 6 5 4 3 2 1

ISBN: 978-1-911508-0-45
eBook ISBN: 978-1-911508-0-52

Proofreader: Sarah Terry; Typesetter: Tetragon, London; Typefaces: Linotype Swift Neue and Verlag; Cover Design: Constance Clavel. Printed and bound by the CPI Group (UK) Ltd, Croydon, CRO 4YY.

A catalogue record for this book is available from the British Library.

This work was published within the framework of the Sur Translation Support Program of the Ministry of Foreign Affairs, International Trade and Worship of the Argentine Republic. Obra editada en el marco del Programa "Sur" de Apoyo a las Traducciones del Ministerio de Relaciones Exteriores y Culto de la República Argentina.

This book was supported using public funding by Arts Council England.

Supported using public funding by
**ARTS COUNCIL
ENGLAND**

MIX
Paper from
responsible sources
FSC® C020471

PETITE FLEUR

Perhaps people never die.
Maybe when dying they hear the name of death
and while it's still ricocheting, the idea of death,
against the sign and notion of death,
life continues on hold.

FOGWILL, HELP A ÉL

This story begins when I was someone else. Like every day since we moved to the town, that Monday morning I got on my bike and started pedalling. Coming out of the tunnel, with the heavy air of the viaduct blowing in my face, it occurred to me that Antonia might remain pint-sized for life. The idea distressed me and at the same time was oddly cheering. That's what I was thinking about on the way uphill, at the exact moment when I noticed a thick column of black smoke leaning against the clouds. Three hundred yards on, at the top of the slope to the industrial park, I could no longer doubt it, the blaze, what remained of the blaze, was coming from the fireworks factory. The premises were surrounded by patrol cars and fire engines. I recognised some of the workers from afar, clustered behind the police cordon. I didn't have the heart to go nearer. I turned around and made for a sizeable tree perched on a hill. I settled at the foot of the trunk to follow events as they unfolded. The swarm of police cars was joined by a few mobile television units. A sort of paralysis gripped me, physical and spiritual. It's impossible to say how long I remained beneath that tree. Encroaching hunger brought me back to earth. I left the scene gnawing on a composite sensation, a mixture of gloom and release. The first few yards I walked beside the bike, so my retreat wouldn't attract suspicion. I called Laura, told her I would be free earlier than usual and suggested we meet under the pergola of the lakeside walk. We'd have a picnic to celebrate Antonia's first birthday. I crossed the drawbridge and sat at a food stall by the canal that was popular with workmen and drivers, where I often went when my thoughts needed tidying. I ordered the dish of the day: roast beef and potatoes. The sight of the mountain of rubbish and the scavengers flapping in circles above it moved me to review the last few years of my life. Somebody once said of me that I was a wonder kid, able to turn anything I touched into gold. I wasted half my life feeling convinced that sooner or later this would come true. The sky cleared, the wind must have changed, the morning's sultriness was dispelled by a refreshing breeze. Our birthday party for Antonia was an intimate, intense occasion. So much so that I vowed to repeat the picnic ceremony until she was grown up. We sat on the steps down to the lagoon and ate white-bread sandwiches, a family favourite. Antonia seemed determined to show us how happy she was, buzzing here and there like a young bee. The way she mesmerised the herons was the clearest evidence of her uncommon life force. Laura and I were moved. That evening, I shut myself in the workshop to finish the doll's house I was making her as a birthday present. I was late with it. All of a sudden the door opened, Laura came in and stood staring, open-mouthed: You didn't tell me! I said I hadn't wanted to upset her on such a special day. I saw the pictures on the news . . . It's a disaster! What are you going to do? I don't know, I said in all sincerity, let's see what happens. I worked late into the night under the stimulus of the paint fumes. I wanted to get the job finished and I did. When I entered the bedroom Laura had fallen asleep with the TV on. A black-and-white movie set in Venice occupied the screen. I turned it off and went online to find out more about the fire. It was everywhere. I read a few reports, theories on how the fire had started, whether due to a short circuit or the explosion of a service-lift fuel tank. There were pictures of the buildings at the end of the day, the devastation was almost total. You could also watch videos taken by local people and motorists at the moment in the small hours when the whole stock blew up: thousands of multi-coloured flares bursting over blackness. The crackling flashes were reminiscent of a far-off, spectacular war. The images inevitably wormed themselves into my dreams. Next day I woke up at the usual time. I showered, dressed, switched on the radio, ate breakfast, and was about to mount my bike when Laura stopped me from the doorway: Where are you going? I wanted to flee, no matter where. I called the firm's various numbers, tried to locate the proprietors on their mobiles, nobody picked up. I entered a catatonic state. Every movement I made seemed false, as though someone had taken over my body and mind. I wandered about the house like a mummy, unhinged, incapable of uttering a word. At night, while Laura slept, I tortured myself by watching clips of the factory blasting into the sky. I watched them obsessively, over and over again. There were shots of every kind and quality, some from the most unusual angles. On Friday the redundancy telegram arrived. Laura reacted coolly, saying that we had to be sensible in the circumstances. She could go back to work; her year off was beginning to feel too long after all. At first, with unthinking conformity, I objected, but the prospect of hunting for a job soon shut me up. Rent and food were non-negotiable expenses. Within the week, Laura went back to the publishing house and I was forced to become a housewife. The initial period was an earthquake. The hours of the day conspired against me, spinning themselves out to underline my uselessness. Worst of all was that dreary stretch in the middle of the afternoon, that sluggish, creeping time between lunch and Laura's return. I entered a black hole in which I could will myself with equal conviction to change the world or to vanish without trace. My spirit had become a permanent hologram. No matter what attitude I tried to take, I'd end up falling into a trap; no initiative ever got beyond the limbo of assertions. Antonia, for whom I'd become indispensable, took over the management of my emptiness. Without her I would have been consumed by depression. Bowing to the evidence after a run of non-existent days, I swapped frustration for negative revolt, abandoning myself to total and deliberate indolence. In my determination to do nothing about anything, time slowed down more. And everyone knows that idleness is the shortest road to filth and moral degeneration. As for Laura, once the novelty had worn off, the working life began to tire her out again, and she started to show impatience with my apathy. After all, she'd had to return to work at the drop of a hat and in tough conditions: two hours there, two hours back, and an inferior position; she'd been demoted from editor to proofreader. You can't let yourself slide like this, she remonstrated. Start with something small, she said one morning before leaving the house. Why don't you tidy up the CDs? We're going to have to some day, even if it's just to bin them. I felt humiliated. Stoically, I shook off the affront, made some extra-strong coffee and settled on the floor with the apple crate where we kept our dust-covered CDs. Piled in an awkward corner of the house, holding out against imminent species extinction, those empty boxes and scratched discs were evidence of a brilliant past, teeming with interests. The task took me all day, and though I'd started off unwillingly, moved entirely by defiant pride, my excitement began to rise from the feet up with almost imperceptible warmth until I couldn't hide it any longer. I don't remember exactly which album it was that clicked, setting off an irresistible urge to hear it again. Probably something by Manal. Or Liszt's rhapsodies. The effect was instantaneous, like a magic trick. Everything was in there! Those neglected discs were where my power lay dormant. Thanks to music I passed from idleness to action, from despondency to hope, and to the ideal management of time. I chose a different album every day, sometimes at random, sometimes intentionally, to set as the rhythm of my movements: opera, blues, folk, rockabilly, and all those bands that had accompanied my adolescence and which I'd consigned to oblivion so very long ago. Thanks to music, by midmorning the house was spotless, lunch was ready and the laundry was drying in the sun. Laura viewed this change of heart as suspect: No need to play the superhero either! I assured her that my energy was genuine. Once I'd cracked the petty jobs, I moved on to the second phase: that of major works. I threw myself into clearing the attic, unblocking the gutters and sorting old clothes for charity. Then I tackled the garden. I started by raking the leaves and mowing the lawn, next I pruned the lemon tree, treated the bark for parasites and laid out a vegetable patch. I bought seeds and bulbs for various kinds of lettuce, garlic, tomato, carrot and beetroot. The first thing to do, according to a gardening manual I found in the library, was make a compost pit to fertilise the soil. And that's how it came about that one Thursday evening around eight o'clock, when Laura got home from work, I went next door to borrow the neighbour's spade. Out on the pavement, with a fabulous moon hung between the jacaranda branches, some lines of a poem my grandmother used to recite came into my mind: *To become a mother | the barren earth needs | some mother's hand to free it | from its litter and weeds.* The neighbour had moved in a few months before, after doing some considerable work on his flat above the pastry shop. The refit had interfered with our lives: the strange hours he kept and the noise of hammering and drilling had woken us more than once. Every day I used to see the builders mixing cement by the kerb. I rang the bell once, twice, no response. At the third ring, the peephole cover swung back. Hello, I live next door, sorry to bother you so late. I explained I wanted to borrow his spade. The door opened and a bright light shone in my eyes. A deeply tanned man in his mid-thirties, wearing jeans and an unbuttoned shirt, was greeting me with a broad smile. He proffered his hand, I pumped it. We introduced ourselves: Guillermo, José. I followed him down a hallway lined with boxes of tiles, rolls of roof insulation and ventilation pipes. The spade stood wedged among bags of sand and lime by the foot of the stairs. We stopped and looked at it without speaking. Guillermo glanced at me with a mischievous grin: You're a music lover. . . It wasn't a question but a statement, in which I couldn't help detecting a reproach. Ever since I'd rediscovered my old sounds I listened to them at all hours and at top volume, never stopping to think whether this could disturb the neighbour. I smiled back sheepishly. But I was wrong, there wasn't the slightest recrimination in his words, rather a strategy for making friends. Come along, he said, the spade forgotten, I have something that might interest you. And I had no choice but to follow. The house was modern in conception, while preserving a classic distribution of space. Each object was in its proper place and everything shone with the gloss of the new: the blacker-than-black screen on the far wall, the white bookcase, the leather kidney-shaped couch, the standard lamp with the flounced tulip shade, the glass-topped coffee table with marble legs and a contrived jumble of art books on the lower level. Guillermo invited me to sit down and offered me a glass of wine. So promptly, it was as if he'd been expecting me. He asked me about myself and I told him a little. I told him about Laura and our little girl Antonia. I lied about my job, saying I was employed by the council. He wanted to know which department. One just being formed, I dodged. He drained his glass and launched forth. I myself, he said portentously, rotating both fore-fingers in the air, am in interior decoration. . . But above all else, what I am is a jazz freak. The phrase gave me the shivers and I took another gulp of the very fine wine he'd poured. From that point on I sank into a hypnotic daze. Guillermo carried on like a magician showing off his tricks. He produced a superb cheese and salami *picada* out of thin air. My palate began to get as worked up as my head. Guillermo presented his record collection: Five hundred and thirty-three jazz albums. It's all here, from A to Z. He made me listen to an endless succession of tracks, the hours fled by faster and faster. At one point, as a honeyed, rhythmic trumpet was sounding, Guillermo started bopping around in the middle of the living room. I was surprised at how relaxed he was. Just look at the time, I said like an automaton, but something had already gone awry inside me . . . and he, with a giggle: Mustn't forget the spade! We staggered downstairs, me behind, hanging on to the banister, Guillermo ahead with a big glass of wine in his hand. On the last step he made a deceptive movement, mumbling something I failed to catch about the spade and the builders. I edged past, offering to shift the sacks that were trapping it. Guillermo shook his head but he couldn't manage either, his glass of wine was in the way and he didn't seem to realise. He squatted down, obviously feeling dizzy, and a slow but raging irritation rose in me. A kind of primitive protest that caused something deep inside to snap. That's when I leaned over, grabbed the spade by the handle and lifted it cleanly from between the bags and in a single continuous motion, up, back and down, sank it into the back of Guillermo's neck. The blade went in far enough to knock his head out of line and with the same momentum again, barely more deliberate, the metal edge reached halfway through his neck. At least that's how it looked to me, although it could have been a lot less than that, or possibly more. The sound of the incision was the most sickening thing about it. Far from falling into a panic, I surveyed the scene meticulously. Instead of gibbering or going to pieces, I felt a sheath of steel grow around my bones from head to toe; at the end of that process I detached my hands from the top of the spade and raised them to either side. It wasn't me, someone, something had taken control of my will. Guillermo was emitting a rosary of short, high-pitched squeaks. The blow had brought him to his knees, arms forward in a reflex attempt to break the fall. A minimal movement compared to the scale of the damage. The odd thing was that whereas the left hand remained on the edge of the bottom step, the other lay palm upward, a beggar. If you ignored the practically severed head, you might think Guillermo was engaged in deep, prayerful supplication, a strange crowning of the whole experience. A furnace heat invaded my ears, preventing me from reacting in any way. I was out of it for I don't know how long, until the squeal of a trumpet from upstairs brought me to my senses. Swallowing back the horror I went for first things first: extract the spade. An odd, final jerk animated Guillermo's torso, tipping his chin on to his chest. The result was a fountain of blood that made me instinctively avert my face. Fortunately, not a single spatter reached higher than my knees. Escape presented itself as a matter of urgency. I made it to the threshold in six strides, still holding the spade. One foot on the pavement, I confirmed the absence of witnesses. The cruellest irony was the temperate air and pristine night. Somewhere out of sight a dray horse's hooves were striking the asphalt. I hurried the short distance between the two buildings, opened our gate, walked to the far end and hid the spade under the hydrangeas. On tiptoes I came in through the back door. The kitchen table was still laid with my supper, long cold, a *pastel de choclo* I'd made myself that afternoon.

I locked myself in the bathroom, avoiding the mirror, removed my trousers, shoes and socks and plunged the lot into the sink, along with what was left of a bottle of bleach. I felt weary in the extreme. And that heat coming from inside. I looked in on Antonia, who was breathing softly, surrounded by her planets. It was a comforting vision and I felt the need to imitate her. Sleep could be a balm, a return to reality. As I entered the bedroom I tripped over the leg of a trestle, sending books and objects crashing to the floor loudly enough to wake any normal person. I didn't bother clearing up but lay down on my side of the bed, face to the invisible ceiling. An involuntary brush against Laura's body aroused her, she began to feel around for me with her toe. To refuse could have elicited suspicion or, worse, a conversation. We made love and Laura sank back into the depths of her porpoise slumber. I wished I could do likewise, in my case the sex had made me more awake. Hardly had my eyes closed than the edge of the spade slicing into flesh came back to me with amazing vividness. My wild thoughts jostled on the edge of delirium for some minutes. I got out of bed decisively, but with no notion of what to do next. As Laura turned over, hugging the pillow, I said to the air: I can't sleep, I'm going to make some tea.

I went into the garden in my underwear and retrieved the spade I'd hidden in the flowerbed. The sky was of a geometric, hallucinatory hue. Greys and blues overlaid each other in defiance of logic. All around, strident and guttural, the chirrups of the cicadas and the cooing of the pigeons combined to increase my befuddlement. Everything seemed so unreal that for a moment I was sure I was in the middle of a nightmare. The illusion didn't last, the bloodstained spade brought me back to earth. I began to dig without further ado, in the exact spot I had intended for the compost pit. As the hole grew deeper I realised I was digging a grave to bury Guillermo. The spade had provided the motive, the murder weapon, and now my deliverance. I dug with the strength of two men, covering myself in mud. I counted thirty-six spadefuls. My years on this earth. Neither grave nor compost pit, what lay before me was a formless morass. I'd often heard it said in the town grocer's that the proximity of the river drew the water table nearer to the surface, and the black sludge at the bottom of the hole offered ample proof of this. I stopped because I was tired out and because it was getting light, the transfigured vault giving way to the unarguable brightness of another dawn. Obviously Guillermo's body could not be moved in daylight. I plunged the spade into the earthen mound, headed straight to bed and lay down beside Laura. Supine, I could no longer master the insane whirling of my mind. When I tried to think back, everything after the moment I hauled myself off his couch to go downstairs disappeared into a black, kaleidoscopic box. Alongside this blurring, an acoustic presence grew steadily more defined: that mellifluous, bewitching music with its inexhaustible beat. And there was I, lifting the spade to gain momentum for a full-on chop at the neighbour's neck. Everything else, including helpless visualisations of the impending scaffold, takes the form of an ordinary drunken night out. Close my eyes and it's that diabolical trumpet again. I wept. And so the day began, with the song of the thrushes drilling into my nerves. Resigned to not sleeping, I waited a decent interval and at the first sounds of morning (a child wailing to be carried, the shrill whistle of the dog walker, a couple of old ladies discussing the poor health of a third), I feigned waking up. Only then did I realise I'd gone to bed slathered in mud from feet to chin. My body was neatly printed on the sheets, like the victim of a shoot-out who's been pulled from a bog and laid by the road. A corpse without a head: the message was eloquent. I struck myself smartly on the forehead with the heel of my hand. Antonia appeared to me, my parental duties, I had to carry on. I shifted Laura with gentle movements so as to remove the dirty sheets, then peered at the street between the slats of the blinds. Nothing seemed amiss, there were no police cars, no officers and no reporters. Who would be the first to find the body? Guillermo was bound to employ a cleaner, the question was whether she went in on Fridays. One of the workmen might drop by to finish a job, the electrician perhaps. Or a client, keen to discuss the details of their new interior decor. Standing in front of the bathroom mirror, I made a vow in exchange for being let off the hook. I opened the cold tap, stripped naked and walked into the shower. Face pressed against the shower head, body still baking hot, I soaped myself lavishly and my eyes were stinging when I heard a baby's cry. I stepped away from the jet with ears pricked. If I was going to sort out my inner fiasco, I had to make sure Laura didn't surface too early. I nearly rushed out dripping wet to quiet Antonia. There was no need, the crying came from outside. Wearing the first garments to hand, a pair of shorts and a white T-shirt, I headed to the kitchen, telling myself to get on top of the situation. Before that I wrung out the clothes I'd left soaking in bleach, bundled them together with the muddy ones and stuffed everything into the machine. As the drum started turning I felt relief for the first time in hours. The soil and grime and blood were irrevocably churned together, it would be hard to reconstruct anything. I switched on the radio and prepared to clean the house. I had to behave naturally. The news concerned a mega train crash in Winnipeg, the death of a young actress, upcoming football matches. Nothing about Guillermo and his beheader. I washed the dishes, mopped the mosaic floor with three squirts of detergent and got breakfast ready: I squeezed every orange in the bowl, scraping the skins dry as though my fate depended on it. Besides the juice I made scrambled eggs and foamy coffee. All this before Laura's alarm was set to go off on her phone. Antonia woke up, whimpering softly. I took her in my arms, changed her nappy and sat her in her high chair in front of some mashed banana. I looked at my hands, could they really be equally good at killing and at caring? Another swift smack to the forehead and I was back in action. I'd found an effective recourse against the contrivances of the mind. It seemed best not to interfere with Laura's routine, and shortly after the alarm rang she strolled out of the bedroom yawning and stretching. She threw us a dazed glance on her way to the bathroom. When she emerged, she remarked on the powerful smell of ammonia coming from the plughole. Bleach, I corrected, I was disinfecting the pipes. How many other clues were ready to incriminate me at the tops of their voices in the most unsuspected places! Laura made to lift Antonia, but the child started whining. This was nothing new, the bond between mother and daughter had deteriorated to a worrying degree ever since Laura had returned to work. Antonia rejected her cuddles, her kisses, even her breast. I made a rueful face, pleading patience. Laura put Antonia back in her chair and glared at me. I've made you a special breakfast, I said to deflect the reproach. Laura went into the bedroom, I sat at the table holding the coffee pot. She took her time composing herself then joined us in silence. I served the eggs and poured her a cup of coffee, she said curtly: No bread? I jumped up, spurred by a frenzy of excitement at this excuse to go outside. To expose myself to the light of day, to contemplate the exterior with my own eyes was surely a good exorcism, a way to stop the madness. I'll go to the pastry shop and be right back, I said. I opened the door, shut my eyes and breathed in deeply. The world was still there, the same as ever. Going past Guillermo's place I checked the grooved pavement without breaking stride, no trace of blood, it hadn't seeped that far. There was an uncommon queue at the baker's. At least six people were ahead of me and it seemed reckless to stand in line for so long, in full view, just for a loaf of bread. I knew I had to make the most of every sign, interpret every wink that came my way, if I weren't to fall conspicuously to pieces. Paranoia began to take over even so. I overheard stray words which I felt sure referred to me: *frightful*, *neighbours*, *inhuman*. But that was the least of it: I was one step from the counter when a shadow tickled my nape. Like a spectral gust licking against the glass. I turned my head just in time to glimpse the tail of a white Kia with polarised windows slide through the reflection of my surroundings. It was unmistakeably Guillermo's car. I knew it well, I'd seen it a thousand times in recent weeks. Always parked in the same place at an angle to the square, bang in the middle of the lot, shiny and mysterious, lording it over the block's other cars. From paranoid circles I'd crashed into the realm of hallucination. I asked for half a kilo of bread like an automaton. The assistant, a plump, rather disagreeable girl I knew by sight, waved the bag in front of my eyes like a talisman. Knock knock, anybody there? I went home in a tremble; Laura was waiting hunched over, cradling her cup. The coffee's cold now, where were you? At the pastry shop or the grain silo? I smiled stupidly, petrified to the core. In between talking about her work or the shopping or the weather, I don't recall, Laura noticed the state I was in and let me know it: Where are you, José? I shook my head several times. It's always hard to maintain an even keel when you live with someone. Antonia got peevish again and started crying. This time Laura turned a deaf ear, made no attempt to soothe her, grabbed her bag and left, flinging an *I'll be home late . . .* over her shoulder. I didn't stop her, not seeing how I could, failing even to wonder what I'd do with Antonia if I were arrested. Everything seemed to be falling unstoppably over a cliff. I had to keep a cool head, trust in everyday things. Whatever I did felt wrong. I sat at the kitchen table with pencil and paper and drew up two lists in a bid to work out the essentials of the situation. It was an infallible device a teacher had shown me for distinguishing right from wrong, truth from lies, action from speculation. Suddenly I heard handclaps outside, I peered through the curtains, my terror subsided when I recognised the roof of the soda van. I handed the crate of empties over the gate and he handed a fresh crate back. Absolute normality. We ate our lunch in silence, eggs and rice. It was past midday and every-thing was as usual. No police, no TV cameras on the doorstep, none of the dreaded scenarios had come to pass. The town was drifting into siesta mode like on the most ordinary of days. Intent on resuming my routine, I put on a Benny Moré disc and got down to the housework. It was time for an in-depth clean under the kitchen counter, where a crusty deposit had built up. I wiped out a cockroach colony, de-rusted the hinges and took the shelves apart, ener-getically enough to break a sweat. The perspiration bucked me up, there was still a chance of twisting the future. Pausing as I scrubbed a troublesome saucepan with steel wool, I looked up and through the smoked-glass pane caught sight of the buried spade, staring back. Like a banner that had lost its cause, an indelible mark of the worst accusation. Countless snapshots, all shuffled together, tumbled through my mind until it blanked out in the phan-tasmagorical wake of Guillermo's car stalking me from behind. I made an effort to finish the cleaning but it was no use, the day entered a painful funnel. Antonia granted me all the forbearance she denied to her mother. I took two siestas in a row, feeling drained. Night came with no news on the neighbour front; Guillermo was decomposing ten yards away from reality. Laura came home later than usual, hollow-eyed and with a whiff of alcohol on her breath. I asked if she was all right: Exhausted, she said, and got into bed with her clothes on. She reached for the remote and switched on the TV. She didn't even ask about Antonia, who had been asleep in her cot for a while. Laura zapped three or four times through the channels without really focusing on anything, a sure sign of fatigue and defeat. What's the neighbour like? she enquired suddenly. I shrugged my shoulders to disguise the skin-prickling shock: Like you'd expect, I don't know . . . we hardly exchanged two words. I ran into him as I came in, he says hi, and she went on jabbing the channel button like a maniac, still not looking at me. Playing with fire. Which neighbour? Are you sure? She didn't answer. I snatched the remote away from her to cut the nonsense short. You're driving me crazy flipping channels, let's stick with something. I plumped for a documentary, just to annoy. *Metamorphosis: From Caterpillar to Chrysalis, From Chrysalis to Butterfly*. The presenter was suggesting in a gravelly voice that metamorphosis, more than any other natural phenomenon, could hold the key to the enigma of life. Laura dozed off, as usual. It was her silent form of protest against the job and the commutes that took so much out of her. I kissed her forehead, wishing I could wake her up, tell her I still loved her, clear this hell out of my head, then at least I'd have a good reason to flee. I couldn't bring myself to do it. I switched off the TV, walked to the window: a white Kia was parked at a 45-degree angle to the square. Could there be two identical cars on this block? An unlikely, though not unthinkable, coincidence. I adjusted the blind to solid blackout. Saturday was a repeat of the previous day, an inner struggle between clinging to my routine and succumbing to the shades of horror that whispered yes and no, no and yes, in ghastly alternation. How could no one have found Guillermo's body yet! At siesta time, goaded by anxiety, I climbed the dividing wall as if to clip some dead wood. I craned my neck to get a view of the next-door terrace; everything was in order, hosepipe looped round the hook, buckets and brooms in a corner, barbecue dismantled, potted ferns and geraniums looking freshly watered. A dragging noise made me jump and almost topple over. A short man in white trousers and a tank top was eyeing me from below while he fed the pigeons in their cage at the back of the bakery yard. Hello, I said, and was about to offer an explanation when he emitted a dog-like snort that spared me the trouble and made me blush. On Sunday I urged Laura to go to the cinema as a tonic. She frowned and grumbled, as if I was pushing this entertainment just to get rid of her, but finally agreed. I bought a paper intending to check the job advertisements, and around five o'clock Antonia and I walked over to the square. We stayed in the sun for a bit, that tepid thin late-summer sun. I kept glancing up furtively at Guillermo's flat, the curtains were drawn and the white Kia was in its usual spot. The mothers and fathers in the playground weren't looking pointedly at me. Dusk fell. The lamps came crackling one by one to life against an ashen sky. Laura whistled at us from across the road, smiling with one hand on the gate, about to go in. Almost without thinking I scooped Antonia up and went to give her to Laura. Spontaneity did the trick, Antonia and Laura seemed to be getting on again. I'll fetch the bucket and tools, I said, Laura blew me a kiss. The movie idea had worked wonders. Walking back across the road I wished I hadn't done quite so much in the past. A pair of twin girls were still at the playground and a boy was pushing their swings in counterpoint, a symmetrical, dynamic composition, very easy on the eye. I located the hole Antonia and I had dug in the sand, knelt down and reached for the rake. And then, just as I lifted my head, I froze. At the window of Guillermo's flat two silhouettes were conversing, face to face behind the curtains. These were not reflections, nor the report of a third person, this time it was actually happening, incontrovertibly, before my eyes. I hurried to collect our things and stationed myself on a bench under the wisteria. One of the figures was angular and chunky, the other rounded and slender, it had to be a man and a woman; they moved with the typical Sunday lethargy that slackens muscles and minds alike. I went hot and cold all over, it was the beginning of the end. They must be a pair of police officers, the prosecutor and an inspector, some relative of Guillermo's, the coroner. And yet their demeanour was too relaxed for people working on a crime scene. They even appeared to be joking together. The night drew on, the heady scent of the blossoms exacerbating my turmoil. From my bench in the square I could also see into our bedroom. Laura and her nocturnal habits: order and television. I thought about Antonia, so soon to be made fatherless. When my gaze shifted back, one of the shadows had vanished, the other was facing in my direction. Definitely a woman. She lit a cigarette, its tip a red dot that swelled and shrank. I felt dread, terror, immense emptiness. The other shape appeared behind the first, now they formed a single shadow in what looked very much like an embrace. Laura's bedside lamp went off, the screen flickered like lightning against the window, they faced each other and began to kiss. As if before a split-screen projection, I was witnessing two simultaneous but contradictory realities. On a single, horrifyingly clear plane a few yards away, sanity and madness had divided my consciousness between them. A taxi pulled up outside Guillermo's. The driver got out, polluting the air with a music whose thudding bass jangled the bakery windows, and he rang the bell. He said something into the entryphone before returning to his place behind the wheel, with a snakeish glance at me in passing, as though my solitude were suspect. A couple of minutes later Guillermo's front door opened and out came a girl with straight fair hair almost down to her waist, clad in leggings and a tight top. She got into the taxi, rolled down the window and poked her hand out to wave. The car moved off, turned right at the corner and disappeared; at Guillermo's the lights stayed on a while, then everything went dark. I clicked my fingers repeatedly to silence the crazed hypotheses crowding into my mind, and stumbled to my feet to go home. Laura was in an expansive mood, sitting on the edge of the bed painting her toenails. She started telling me about the movie she'd seen, the story of two Korean girls who fall for the same man and decide to share, without him cottoning on. She described an outdoor sex scene in some sort of botanical garden with ponds, bridges and cherry trees in blossom, which instantly aroused me. I didn't let her finish, kissed her, we undressed and made love tenderly and furiously by turns. All the time I couldn't stop picturing those two figures entwined by the window. On Monday I relapsed into paralysis. I moped listlessly all day, racked by uncertainty. Antonia was forced to put up with a father lost in a labyrinth, an image that would be imprinted on her for life. The survival instinct instructed me to compare mirages with realities. I waited for Laura to come home, and told her: I'm going to return the neighbour's spade. My unconscious was betraying me with the utmost perfidy. How could I possibly court my own disgrace, which would just as much be hers? Laura shrugged, she seemed low again; a day at the office had nipped her recovery in the bud. This job wasn't doing her any good. I went out to the street, took three steps backwards and looked up to see Guillermo's lights were on, like the previous evening. It was double or quits. I pressed the bell and waited. Shaking, aghast at the situation, proud of my bravery. The response was immediate. Coooming! called a voice wreathed in tinny echoes. The hints of the last few days had braced me for something uncanny, but even so, when the door opened I couldn't stifle a giggle of dismay. I tried to cover it by clapping my hands, as if applauding the final flourish of a superior circus act. Guillermo greeted me with a beaming smile, elated to the point of euphoria. Sorry about the time, I said, fluttering my fingers by the side of my head to justify the giggle. I dropped my eyes to the floor between his feet, the hallway was intact, not a stain to be seen. At the foot of the stairs, as I ascertained over his shoulder, bags of sand and lime were still copiously piled. Guillermo turned his head to follow my gaze, swaying like a cartoon boxer. How could I tell him, how was I supposed to explain that four days ago I had left him in that very corner with his head half off? Because there was no disputing that Guillermo was in rude health, tan topped up and an extra shine in his eye. He wore a rugby shirt with broad black-and-white stripes and the number 34 on the back. You're being weird, he challenged, what's wrong with you? Anyone would think you'd seen a ghost! The hackneyed phrase calmed me. I let out a frank, cathartic guffaw, and took advantage of the jollity to pat him on the shoulder. This contact, our first since the events of that night, operated like the classic pinch on the cheek. You're something else, he concluded, rearranging his forelock with a precise toss of the head, and invited me upstairs. Don't just stand there, come on up. Unable to refuse, I walked behind Guillermo like a zombie. To discover I was innocent came as a relief, yet at the same time it was terribly unsettling. I hung back at the scene of the crime for a few seconds, searching for some clue to what had happened. There was absolutely nothing, not the faintest trace of last Thursday's carnage. Just a tiny gash, like a child's lip, at the bottom of one of the sand bags. Guillermo beckoned from the landing, impatient to show off his latest acquisition: a smartbar. A Japanese friend had brought one over for him and he'd just finished assembling it. Let's try it out, he enthused. Guillermo had an overwhelming personality. Never letting up, physically or mentally, he unleashed a barrage of music and histrionics. He chattered incontinently, whipping himself into a fever over the slightest thing. He appeared to view life as a hedonistic adventure. Near midnight, he put on another version of the same syrupy tune as last time and began jiggling his shoulders to the beat. His severed head invaded my mind, I felt the power again, the limitless rage. Just look at the time, I said hastily, and he: Come on, don't be shy. As I fled I could hear him laughing behind me. I hadn't had a moment to think, I needed somebody, a voice of reason, to corroborate or to deny everything. At home, silence and darkness reigned. The first thing I did was check whether the spade was still in the garden. There it stood, next to the pit without a purpose. No use looking for traces of blood, the soil and rain had already taken care of these. The past no longer mattered, the nightmare was here and now. Laura lay sound asleep, I stretched out beside her, my head wouldn't let me alone. Once more I tried to make sense of what had happened. It was one thing to suspect that Guillermo was alive after seeing him dead as a doornail, and quite another to find this confirmed. Discarding bad dreams or hallucinations, I masturbated twice, coming to terms with the possibility that my neighbour was one of the elect. Though it was odd for such an ordinary man to possess a gift like that. Next morning I woke up determined to crack the mystery, and prepared to carry out a series of experiments with death that would yield astounding results. I began with an ant. I selected a big one, the most strapping of the group that was carrying a piece of mulberry leaf back to the nest. I placed it on a broken tile and squashed it good and flat under my big toe. I observed the inert insect for a while, then forgot about it. The seeds I'd bought a few weeks back were still in their wrappers on a shelf, as was the green plastic fence intended to protect the vegetable patch. That project had been interrupted; now was the moment to return to it, which would surely bring out the best in me. Sustenance for the present and a legacy for my daughter. A short time later, making furrows for the seeds, I passed the broken tile and noticed the ant had gone. That didn't mean a thing, it could have been eaten by a spider or a frog, or it could simply have blown away. If it had been resurrected, I could never hope to distinguish it from its hundreds of fellows. I allowed that this test was inconsequential, anyone can kill an ant; I would have to do something more definitive by taking bigger risks. The solution was in plain view. I raised my eyes and saw the aviary over the wall. Having overheard some confidential exchanges between the owner of the pastry shop and his sporting associates, I knew the pigeons were entered for various competitions. The caged ones were mostly laying females, while the superior specimens were housed at the homing pigeon club. I also knew from simple observation that they were let out on Saturday mornings. They seldom strayed, being too fat to fly properly. The club members would gather for an improvised auction that ruined the customary peace and quiet of the neighbourhood. I hatched a plan for the following Saturday. I bought a bag of birdseed and sprinkled some over the grass, supposedly to entertain Antonia. Overfed though they were, a couple of pigeons were bold enough to investigate. Food in unwonted places is always tempting. There was an instant contagion effect. The garden filled with pigeons pecking greedily around Antonia's feet, like a typical cathedral postcard but at home. Against her will Laura was attending a creative away day on a farm, organised by her employers. They want to set up an ideas bank, she spat, as if the words were a mouthful of something nasty. When Antonia's back was turned, I donned a gardening glove and seized a pigeon by the neck as surreptitiously as possible. Fortunately I was wearing one of those sweatshirts with a roomy front pocket where I could hide the bird. It wriggled no matter how tightly I held it. I crossed the garden and entered the workshop. Quickly, blindly, I crammed the pigeon into the shoebox where I kept brushes and cutters and sealed it up with packing tape. From Saturday noon to Sunday night I kept thinking about that bird, the wrongful captivity I'd imposed on it. Guillermo had never died at all, this was stress, eating into me and sapping my faculties. The solution was to put shame aside and lay my case before a psychiatrist. On Monday morning I sprang up raring to carry out the experiment, my previous misgivings forgotten. While Antonia was having her mid-morning nap, I rolled up my sleeves. The pigeon was still alive, though much debilitated. I grasped it by the neck again and took it to a corner of the yard by the wall, where I administered a clean blow to the head with a brick. That did it. The blood trickling from beak and eyes certified its demise. I felt sullied, but with this I had at least rid myself of magical notions, proved that the ant had been blown away by the wind and that my story with Guillermo was nothing but a chimera spawned by idleness. A clear and piercing wail roused me from my thoughts. Antonia was crying, or pretending to, at the top of the steps leading down to the garden. I went to pick her up and as I approached with arms outstretched saw her face change from fear to delight. I turned my head to follow the direction of her gaze at the very moment the pigeon I had just bludgeoned, my pigeon without a doubt, took off from the ground and flew in a perfect parabola towards the aviary. My stupefaction turned to horror and that horror into a strange sense of potency that somehow had to do with love. I hugged Antonia hard. I love you so much! I said, kissing her all over. I possessed a power, an absurd and wonderful power. After a few days I realised that solving the enigma meant facing Guillermo again. Habit calls to habit like the planets call to the sun. That Thursday, when Laura returned from work, I delivered the daily update (Antonia's asleep, there's chicken and rice in the pan), prowled unnecessarily about the house for a bit and halted near the door, deliberately repeating: I'm going to return the neighbour's spade. Laura shrugged and let me go without comment. I rang the bell and this time Guillermo didn't come down, he whistled from the window and threw me the keys inside a sock. The encounter unfolded along the same lines as the previous two occasions: me reclining on the leather couch, Guillermo fluttering about seeing to the music and the drinks. He asked about the vegetable patch, I explained it was still more of an aspiration; he wanted to know about Laura, what her star sign was, how we'd met; he told me about his projected trip to Europe, and mentioned his knotty relationship with his mother and sister. He said: I got to where I am from scratch. I don't owe anything to anyone. Under the influence, the conversation became amusingly coarse. Guillermo changed his shirt and I found myself wondering if I was capable of committing the crime again. The answer came with the music, an orchestrated version of my host's favourite tune. Here was my cue. Just look at the time, I stammered, as Guillermo started dancing on the coffee table. One thing led irreversibly to the next. I opened my eyes and dimly saw a knife block behind the counter. A chain of smiles took me into the kitchen. Guillermo danced on imperviously, I drew out a long knife that looked sharp, concealed it against my leg and backed out. I waited for Guillermo to complete a pirouette and, when he faced me again, drove the steel blade into the middle of his chest. Just as when the spade had sunk into his neck, the most shocking thing about the blow was the sound it made. Brief and muted yet explosive, like a wave smashing against a rock. But it came from the sternum, not the ocean. I left him on his back on the floor, gurgling blood. Again the adrenaline revolutionised my body, and yet I felt easier. Partly for luck and partly due to the incomparable lust that violent death arouses, I took Laura on an acrobatic sex voyage that lasted till dawn. There was no suspense this time. I jumped out of bed early the next morning and rushed to Guillermo's, with the excuse of having forgotten my glasses. It was unnecessary. The door stood wide open. The stout woman who was mopping the hall informed me that the gentleman had already left for work. I decided to take a break from experimenting with my gift and began to research the topic of resurrection. From the epistles of Paul of Tarsus ('And if Christ be not risen, then is our preaching vain, and your faith is also vain') to the Book of Isaiah ('Thy dead men shall live, together with my dead body shall they arise. Awake and sing, ye that dwell in dust'), from Mayan beliefs to the Lazarus syndrome, from Tolkien's fantasies to zombie literature, from metempsychosis to series about ghosts, I got myself into a hopeless muddle. Guillermo's case was so different from all the rest! He didn't ascend to heaven or grow a pair of wings, there didn't appear to be any consequences, nor did this herald the end times. That evening, after floundering in confusion for hours, I glimpsed what had been lying right under my nose though never in plain sight: Resurrection! Suddenly the word made sense, and I raced to the library. I hunted along the shelves for the thick volumes of Tolstoy that had been my staff and guiding light during the

glory years of youth. I soon spotted the unmistake-
able blood-red spines, the cherished objects with
their titles stitched in gold thread. The scent of old
leather, the silky-smooth texture of the yellowing
pages, the crawling in my fingertips, at once propelled me back to happiness. That period between
the ages of fifteen and eighteen, though I was reading
much less than I claimed and spouting shamelessly
about what I hadn't read, nonetheless saw my
entrance into the higher realms of literature.
Surrounded by books, I walled myself in against the
looming menace of adulthood. Books, books and
more books, lying in heaps, piled into pointless
towers, littering the floor, overflowing the shelves.
Resurrection had become my emblematic novel
because I loved it, but also, I admit, because of a
certain snobbery. The fact that it was so much less
well-known than *War and Peace* or *Anna Karenina*
endowed me with the status of a pioneer among my
little band of pubescent bookworms. Feeling an urge
to share this reunion with someone, I went to find
Antonia, who was sitting on the rug in her room,
gnawing on wooden blocks, and read her the first
paragraph aloud: *Though hundreds of thousands had
done their very best to disfigure the small piece of land on
which they were crowded together, by paving the ground*

with stones, scraping away every vestige of vegetation,
cutting down the trees, turning away birds and beasts, and
filling the air with the smoke of naphtha and coal, still
spring was spring, even in the town. Of course I remembered it! Beautiful and true. Spring will be spring
forever! The idealism of the text reflected its lament,
that's what made it so moving. Antonia gazed into
my eyes, subscribing to every word: . . . *the flies were
buzzing along the walls, warmed by the sunshine. All were
glad, the plants, the birds, the insects and the children.* The
message would not defer to aesthetic virtue: *But men,
grown-up men and women, did not leave off cheating and
tormenting themselves and each other. It was not this spring
morning men thought sacred and worthy of consideration,
not the beauty of God's world, given for a joy to all creatures,
this beauty which inclines the heart to peace, to harmony,
and to love, but only their own devices for enslaving one
another.* A shiver went through me. It was still a
marvellous passage. It didn't advance the plot, or
introduce the characters, or set up an imbroglio,
and yet it conveyed the very marrow of the story.
Of every story! Antonia interpreted my tremor and
gifted me with a smile at once loving and detached,
knowing but without malice, full of complicit irony,
the kind that builds the great bridge linking each
generation to the next. That night I reread the first

ten chapters at a sitting, carried away by the same
Russian fever that had infected me as a teenager.
Besides Tolstoy, for whom I professed an obsessive
devotion (I'd pinned a photo of his woodland tomb
above my bed, like a talisman for the night), I also
enjoyed reading Dostoevsky (at one point there were
four different translations of *Crime and Punishment*
in my bookcase), Chekhov (the poet Trigorin was
my kindred soul), Gorky's *The Mother*, Turgenev's
strange tales, and the great Mayakovsky. My private
hero, my other great weakness. I worshipped this
harsh, austere, romantic character; I used to recite
some of his poems off by heart: *Listen! | If the stars
are lit up, | Does that mean somebody needs them? | That
someone wants to see lit up | Every night above the roofs |
At least one star?* Later, courtesy of Antosh, the cook
at the Ukrainian Association, I discovered Sergei
Yesenin. According to Antosh, who deplored
Mayakovsky as a sentimentalist and a demagogue,
Yesenin was a poet in the proper sense, an interpreter
of revolution and nature. His work is certainly force-
ful and vigorous, but Mayakovsky was, for me,
beyond compare. Though it's true I've always been
easy prey for sentiment and demagoguery. I didn't
have the same passion for authors from the Soviet
era. Never really appreciated Solzhenitsyn, and

couldn't finish *In The First Circle*. The Slavonic influence coloured my first clumsy endeavours under
the auspices of the Plaza Eleven writing workshop.
I Russified the stories, the characters and the language. I dealt in snowy landscapes, patronymics and
Tsarist journals. I even attempted a rewrite of *The
Gambler* from the viewpoint of a young regular at
the roulette table, I've probably got a copy of that
somewhere. My fanaticism did not stop at fiction: I
had become an inveterate Russophile. I found a
bronze samovar with wooden handles in a junk shop
and put it on my desk. It looked handsome but didn't
quite fulfil its function, it leaked onto my books and
papers and ruined them. I'd also got hold of a Soviet
army greatcoat, which occupied pride of place in
my wardrobe. I looked forward to those raw winter
days when I could go for a stroll downtown, visit a
cinema or café, take the metro, all in the garb of a
Muscovite soldier. But there was one thing missing
for my vocation to be complete: the language. One
of my greatest ambitions was to speak or at the very
least read Russian, free at last from the veil of translations. I tried to teach myself, using a textbook for
children which a friend's father had brought from
Kiev. The first pages featured illustrations which I
never tired of looking at: a nursery school packed

with toddlers, the cupolas of St Basil's Cathedral, a space rocket exhibition, the ballerinas of the national theatre, a youth camp on the shores of a lake. Thanks to that book I learned to recognise and decipher the Cyrillic alphabet, but it soon became obvious that I wasn't going to get very far on my own. So it was that one afternoon in March I caught a bus to the Argentine Society for Russian Culture, and signed up for a course. My initial enthusiasm was so great that within a few weeks, guided by a severe, garishly made-up teacher, I dared to tackle some lines of Pushkin in the original. How indescribably satisfying! My impetus flagged the more we delved into the intricate business of declensions: the genitive and suchlike got the better of my feeble adolescent's perseverance. It was a short-lived episode, but so intense that the benefits and repercussions are still with me, for good and for ill. I lasted three or four months, long enough to master expressions such as the all-purpose *pozhaluysta*, the indispensable *ya ne ponimayu po-russki*, and, most essential of all, the *ya tebya lyublyu* that I mentally addressed to Anika during all those lonely, insomniac nights. Because while my attempt at learning Russian was ultimately frustrated, it did get me falling in love. Anika was employed by the society to collect fees, sell study aids and make photocopies. She also ran the small souvenir shop: maps, CDs, *matryoshkas*, miniature Kremlins. At first all I saw in her was a galumphing girl with oval glasses and a dopey look. Hi, *spasibo*, bye, that was it. Until one day, in what was perhaps my last act of faith in language acquisition, I went to buy an exercise book. She smiled and rose to fetch it from a shelf, and my vision of the world changed. Her presence shattered the logic of time and space. How come I'd never noticed her! I went on attending for Anika's sake, having relinquished all hope of making progress. Cases and endings streamed through my ears like pure abstractions; the one thought in my head was that after class I would linger in her office on some administrative or academic excuse. Anika intimidated me with her bearing, her self-satisfied eyes and the experience I imputed to her. The four or five years between our ages were enough to make me suppose her out of reach. When exam time came I knew I couldn't keep up the pantomime and stopped attending lessons, but I paid the fees for a further two months merely to see and talk to her. I killed the time in a nearby arcade full of costume-hire shops, erotic boutiques and camouflage-gear outlets. Just before it closed, I'd enter the society building with the small hope of mustering the nerve to invite her for a drink. One day while writing out my receipt, she flashed me a challenging look over the rim of those mousy, provocative librarian's glasses she affected: Why do you keep on paying, when you don't go any more? I quailed like a little animal. It was now or never. Scraping up valour from the pit of my stomach: Would you like to have dinner with me . . . one of these days? Sure, she said, why not? It was that easy. We made a date for the following Friday. Outside the institute, the infernal traffic, the lighted shopfronts of Avenida Rivadavia and the hairdos of elderly ladies seemed like the native flora of some exotic forest of dreams. That evening I understood that what we believe to be impossible is apt to lie three seconds away. The rendezvous was at nine o'clock in the Ukrainian Society, an old mansion with round tables, folksy table linen and tourist posters. I sat and waited for a good half hour, long enough to decide I'd been naive. Not at all, she turned up in memorable style, wearing a thigh-hugging skirt and a satin blouse that accented her nipples. The makeup verged on caricature. I stood up. Antosh, the chef and the life and soul of the place, intercepted her with a bear hug, kissing her on the lips so effusively that I went back to my chair. My role was unclear to begin with. Anika barely let me see the menu, she ordered borsch, blinis, *vareniki* and white wine. Having yearned so intensely for this moment, I now felt completely at a loss. I was nervous, the conversation kept petering out, I could think of nothing but inanities to say. Anika started talking about hands, how important they were for knowing the other and oneself. Show us, she said, extending hers. Its shadow loomed over my hand like a low-hanging storm cloud, a mother ship. You've got small hands, she ruled, with a smile at once sweet and salacious. The drink helped me quell my discomfort and put forward my funniest, friendliest self. I focused on her, asking questions. Anika expounded on the art of decorating *matryoshkas*, she had learned it at school and now practised at home. The dolls came from China, and on a productive evening she could paint half a dozen. I said loudly: Wouldn't I like to see those dolls naked! Anika laughed heartily, and it felt like I was taking back the reins of the night. My self-respect was restored. Antosh himself brought the dessert, a chocolate-coated goat's milk cheesecake, and sat down between us with a bottle of craft vodka. He obviously didn't like me, and made no attempt to conceal his jealousy. Anika told him I was keen on Russian literature. He sneeringly enquired about my favourite authors, and when I mentioned Mayakovsky he puckered in disgust and launched into a fanatical paean to Yesenin. By the end of the meal I was drunk as a newt, as befits a novice. I nevertheless managed to steer Anika towards her house. On the way we sat in a dark square in front of a building with flags on it, and there we kissed for the first time. A fabulous kiss of both depth and duration. We couldn't contain ourselves. Anika stroked my bulge through my trousers while I felt her tits between her ruffles. She invited me up to her flat: So I can show you the naked *matryoshkas* . . . We went on groping each other in the lift. The first sight on coming through the door was a scaled-down jungle. Half the living room was given over to a greenhouse in which Anika kept thirty or so potted plants under infrared lamps. It took me a while to accept that these were marijuana plants, I'd never seen anything like it, didn't know such a thing existed. Anika took the lead. She didn't give me a minute to sit down or find out more about the plantation. She did it all: stripped me, sucked me, rode me, used me like a glove. Her skin broke out in rashes all over. We smoked her crop between coupling and coupling, the grand total, unless my memory has run away with itself, was nine fucks, the last with the sun shining full on us. Anika was highly verbal during sex, half in Russian and half in Spanish, a funny Spanish between baby talk and street slang. She gave instructions, sang, begged voraciously for my come. She called my penis a dicky bird, like she was a child or an old lady. While I wasn't strictly speaking a virgin, and I'd smoked the odd joint, what I experienced that night more than surpassed everything I'd known before and much of what would come later. Sleep buried me. Minutes earlier, semi-conscious, I heard her say: Sex is better than life. When I awoke it was almost noon and Anika wasn't there. She had left me a note signed with a lipstick kiss, saying she'd gone to fetch some cousins from the airport. I spent a couple of hours roaming the flat between cannabis plants, paint pots and the *matryoshkas* awaiting a coat of varnish. Small spaces are more tempting to explore than large ones, and the same goes for people. I wasn't sure if I was supposed to wait or not, but didn't feel like meeting the Ukrainian cousins. Hunger prevailed in the end and I left, confident we'd soon meet up again. I was wrong. I called her the next day and the next, all week long, but a hoarse, threatening male voice answered every time, forcing me to hang up. At last I went to see her at the Russian Culture society.

Anika received me stonily and ushered me to the landing on the stairs. I'd rather not see you any more, she said brusquely. Stop calling, it gets me into trouble. She turned her back and stalked off with giant strides. Five or six years later we happened to be on the same bus. I could hardly believe it was her with that dyed orange hair, abstracted gaze, dark bags under the eyes. The sight of her huge hand resting on the back of a seat put paid to any doubts. We travelled like two strangers for the space of half an hour, just a few bodies apart. I never saw her again. Anika's hand has visited me ever since, in dreams and in real life. Crushing yet protecting me, like a sacred palm poised to dispense loving care and punishment alike. Taking a break from recent events helped me to resume my visits to Guillermo in a different spirit. Every Thursday, when Laura got home, we would engage in what I privately called 'the domestic waltz', which included the daily report on Antonia and supper; a choreography of brief steps that ended with Laura sitting at the table and me standing by the door. Then I say: I'm going to return the neighbour's spade. Laura hunches her shoulders, looks down and dully begins to push her food around with her fork. I leave the house, lingering awhile in the street to sample the night. When I ring the bell

Guillermo drops the keys from the window, wrapped in a sock. Here, too, albeit in a different mode or a different idiom, there was a routine. We drank wine, vermouth and whisky, we snacked to the strains of jazz. Conversation was the least of it. I remained on the couch while Guillermo marched restlessly up and down, fretting about the inadequacy of my musical culture: You've got these awful gaps. And then he'd start, not very methodically, to play records and name styles. When we were both pretty drunk, me more than him, or sometimes the reverse, I'd say at some point: Just look at the time! Guillermo would demur, before putting on yet another version of his fetish song. That melody, so familiar to me by now, signalled the climax, the cue for me to swing into action. One night, anticipating the scene, I asked him about the tune he always played at the end. He told me it was called 'Petite Fleur', a classic composition from the fifties by Sidney Bechet, the most celebrated vibrato jazz had ever known. He was as talented as Louis Armstrong but not as lucky. Too black for the whites and too white for the blacks, that was his karma. Guillermo had collected 125 different versions, some that were subtle variations, others that amounted to veritable rewrites, by everyone from Bechet himself to Fausto Papetti, as well as rockers and crooners: *Of that love, that old blue dream of mine, all that's left, little flower, is you.* Anyhow, as soon as that tune kicked off, Guillermo would dim the lights and begin to sway, coaxing me to join in: Come on, don't be shy! From that point on everything was up to me, I had to act before the music ended: such was the unspoken watchword, the fundamental rule of the game. A partly conscious game that initiated a twofold duel, between my thoughts and my actions and between my actions and the circumstances. I had sworn never to plan or to repeat the method, the important thing was to be swift, unerring and lethal. I hit him on the head with a marble bust, I slashed his carotid artery, I throttled him with a fishing line, quite vindictively on occasion, or else with solicitude, anything went, it was a matter of inspiration. I went as far as kicking him to death, in the face, in the balls, in the ribs: kick kick kick. Before withdrawing I always paused a moment to contemplate the final tableau. My work done and the music soaring behind me, I walked out to meet the night. Famished for sex, more alive than ever. It all came to grief when Laura started rejecting me, having entered a calamitous downward spiral. She found the proofreading work demeaning, the relationship with her daughter excruciating, and the commute to and from the city completely draining. Doing my best to empathise, I suggested she should give herself more 'me' time. Maybe by going to read a book in a café, or taking an aimless walk, or having a long soak in the bath, she would regain her lost self-esteem. Or perhaps she should do something with her body: yoga, gymnastics, swimming. She would slap down every suggestion with a sarcastic remark and change tack: Easy for you, she'd say, sitting on your arse all day long. I did my best to placate her, but at the third or fourth time she insisted on being offensive, I would snap and fling in her face all the domestic jobs I had to do. The cleaning, the bills, the garden, the shopping, the cooking. Not to mention what it took to look after Antonia, who couldn't be left alone for a second. This last wasn't quite true, though it sounded plausible. Antonia possesses a rare, precocious sense of independence. You can be perfectly oblivious to her for long stretches at a time without incurring the slightest risk. What's more, when she can see I'm busy with something, like sweeping the floor or changing a washer, she becomes more self-sufficient still, which engages a virtuous circle of positive influences. Her accomplishments come into their own when I take her to the square. Whereas the other children, often older than her, demand assistance from grandparents, parents or nannies to play in the sandpit, Antonia handles her own bucket, spade and rake and gets on with digging wells, making paths or building castles all by herself. Some mothers show amazement at her cleverness, earning gratified smiles from me. This can become the pretext for a conversation, which were I to go with the flow could lead to something more. As an old friend used to say, there's no bait like a brat if you're looking to pull. Returning to Laura and her moods, she kept harping on about the boredom of the office, the frightful texts she was forced to read like a slave, the endless hours on public transport, the whole miserable package. Proofreading is hell, she said. Worse than hell! I played the self-denying saint. The argument would end in deadlock, neither of us was living in accordance with our desires, frustration was the order of the day. Though we never spoke it aloud, the word *separation* hovered over us like a cloud of flies, buzzing at every step. Matters came to a head one day when in the heat of a quarrel Laura threw a glass at me, which I managed to sidestep before it crashed into a picture frame. A photo of the two of us on the deck of a catamaran at the beginning of our romance. Laura shut herself in the bedroom to cry, I slumped onto a kitchen chair, downing whisky after whisky. I needed relief, and my thoughts turned to Guillermo. I quickly put my shoes on and went over: it was a Monday or a Tuesday, I think, the first time I'd broken our routine. I rang the bell, but there was no answer. And yet from across the road I could clearly see the lights were on, and the shadow-play of a group of silhouettes writhing behind the curtains. Dancing, perhaps? I felt jealous of those other people who hung out with Guillermo on the nights I didn't see him. Deflated, I watched them for some time from the square: bobbing heads, fits of laughter, so many signs of cheer. I came home crushed. Laura was still in our room, I tried the door but she'd locked it, and to cap it all she'd fallen asleep with the TV on. I curled up on the sofa, forced to listen to movie soundtracks and ads until morning. Things went from bad to worse. It was during this period of deep crisis that Horacio appeared. A saviour and a fiend rolled into one. On the train coming back from the city one evening Laura ran into Marion, an old friend from secondary school. And not just any old friend, more precisely a former guiding light and role model for the many girls who were, like Laura, just reaching puberty and extending feelers towards sex and life.

Laura did her best to avoid her, she was in no state for catching up with someone whose story she assumed to be brilliant and successful. The polar opposite of her own. Marion had been the prettiest girl of the class by far, unfair competition for other hopefuls at parties. Invariably gorgeous even when not dolled up, she danced, thought and dressed like no one else. Laura was drowsing against the window when Marion boarded the train wearing headphones. She looked the same, a little more ravaged. Laura recognised her at once and pretended to be miles away, taking refuge in one of those bestsellers with embossed covers they gave out for free at work. Until at some moment, instinct or treachery, treachery and instinct, she lifted her eyes straight into Marion's, who reacted with disproportionate joy. The intensity of the embrace aroused Laura's suspicions. The seat opposite came free and they travelled together to the terminus. Laura summed up her situation trying to paint it in a positive light, she spoke about me, Antonia, the move, her job. Marion lived alone in a small apartment, she had dated a lot of men, none had lasted more than a year, she had gone through a lesbian phase and had travelled the world to the point of boredom. But she wasn't twenty or even thirty any more, and some time ago, when her last boyfriend left her to go back to his ex, months after they'd started living together, she became severely depressed. She felt like an emotional cripple, unable to love or be loved. This bad patch encompassed suicide attempts, pills and psychiatric referrals. Leaving the train, they moved on to a bar. Laura had coffee while Marion continued to unburden herself between swigs of black beer. The hell of drug addiction was not a cliché, she had experienced it in here, she said, thumping her chest with her fist, there were nights when she didn't know where she had gone to bed or with whom, she hardly ate, underwent a string of abortions, life had bulldozed her. Softened up by the confessions of her much idealised friend, Laura poured out her own troubles. She described the stress that was consuming her in body and mind, our constant bickering, and above all her fraught relationship with Antonia. She had always wanted a child, and now all she got was rebuffs. Nothing but let-down. Laura burst into tears and found unexpected comfort in her adolescent rival. Marion revealed that she was getting better: after trying out all kinds of treatment, she had alighted on a therapy group run by a certain Horacio. They met on Wednesdays at a studio on Calle Defensa, opposite Parque Lezama, on the very same block where we had lived for so long. I encouraged her to give it a whirl. It'll be a bit like going home, Laura said with a forlorn smile. The sessions began at eight and you never knew what time they would finish. I used to wait up, not so much worried something might happen to her as seized by an abrupt fear of loss. I felt better as soon as I heard the squeak of the gate. Laura would come in and sit on the side of the bed, eager to tell me how the session had gone. On one of her first times, the spotlight had been on Marion. In the darkness of our room, her voice breaking, deeply affected, Laura related what had happened. Marion had talked about her dark years, her disappointments in love, her current loneliness and the stigma of attractiveness she found so painful: I don't want to be Marion for the rest of my life! Horacio sent her into the middle and made her undress. Clothes off, he said peremptorily. And when she hesitated to remove her bra and pants: The lot! He circled round, inspecting her close up: She doesn't look all that attractive to me . . . What do you guys think? He cruelly ticked off every defect in her body, the pimple on the forehead, the undersized bottom, the stretch marks on the waist; he pointed to the incipiently sagging breasts and protruding navel, and added that the face was downright common in his view. And what about that stringy yellow hair, like an ageing Barbie doll. Time for a trim, Horacio announced, chose a young man at random, handed him a pair of scissors and instructed him to chop off Marion's hair any old how. The man obeyed. After that the group members, including Laura, filed past to insult her, which some did with incredible venom. They spat, they kicked, they called her *you piece of shit, you whore, you dirty slut*. Horacio forced her to piss herself in front of everyone. Curled in the foetal position, Marion obeyed and started weeping over the puddle of her own urine. Laura couldn't bear it, she added her tears to her friend's in the midst of a general horrified silence. No one dared to rebel. Horacio went over to Marion, pulled her to her feet with one hand and wrapped a towel around her. Magic! he cried, flinging both arms wide in an arc, like a conjurer. Marion gradually calmed down and joined the others again. At the end of the session Horacio urged her to continue the performance on her own, making herself as ugly as possible for a week. That way she would finally be able to cast off her untrue self. I could hardly believe my ears, and wondered momentarily whether Laura was exaggerating just to wind me up. After that some of the group went for a drink at the Bar Británico. Marion said she was somewhat in shock but not too bad, she'd have to process the experience, in theory she felt lighter already. Laura confided to me, not without residual jealousy, that while they were in the bar, despite the way Marion had allowed herself to be unspeakably degraded in front of everyone, those same men who had humiliated her half an hour before now coveted her. Ugly and all, she was still their first choice. I thought two things, which I kept to myself. One, some physiques are not easily spoiled. The other was that Laura nursed a historic envy of Marion that no amount of time could erase. Days later, unable to get the scene out of my mind, I remembered the drama of the lovely Marcela, who also believed herself doomed by the gaze of others: 'The beauty I possess was no choice of mine, for, be it what it may, Heaven of its bounty gave it me without my asking or choosing it; and as the viper, though it kills with it, does not deserve to be blamed for the poison it carries, as it is a gift of nature, neither do I deserve reproach for being beautiful; for beauty in a modest woman is like fire at a distance or a sharp sword; the one does not burn, the other does not cut, those who do not come too near.' Contrary as she was, Laura became a fanatic of Horacio's therapy sessions, from which she came home exhilarated or distraught. Never unaffected. And she needed me and my amazement, needed a listener on whom to unload her emotions. It wasn't exactly a reconciliation, but in some sense Horacio brought us closer together. His figure so grew in stature that it became an obligatory reference in all our conversations. Every subject, from the most trivial to the most profound, was an opportunity for Laura to bring up Horacio and one of his magical solutions. I must admit that I, too, became somewhat obsessed. I tried to find out more about him online, and even, I can say this now, in Laura's emails. Actually and no doubt deliberately, to feed his own myth, Horacio shone by his absence. I failed to track down a surname, or to find out whether Horacio was his real name. What I did find was a positive surfeit of data, texts and videos relating to Alejandro Jodorowsky, whose disciple Horacio claimed to be. An elusive, multifaceted character, hard to pin down given how many hats he wears. A psychomagician, a Tarot scholar, a film-maker and a writer, regarded by many as the spiritual guru of the new millennium. I watched one of his movies, *Santa Sangre*, which was in my opinion awful, but impressive. The plot, set in a circus peopled by dwarves, freaks and grotesques, mixes art and politics in a stream of baroque, garbled allegories. Laura stuck his 'Decalogue for Happiness' on the fridge, and at the height of her zealotry wrote some maxims on the walls and doors in indelible marker. One in particular was repeated more than once in an impetuous scrawl: 'The greatest lie is the Ego.' Nevertheless, Horacio was streets behind his supposed mentor in terms of training and creativity. This was finally brought home to me on the night I met him in person. Laura invited me to a Friendship Day dinner in Horacio's studio. Each member of the group was allowed to bring an outsider, their partner or a relative, to share what they had dubbed 'the pre-last supper'. I never did work out what that meant. Despite all our ups and downs, Laura decided to ask me. I must say I was surprised, because she seemed genuinely to want me there. I said thanks, but it would be best if she went on her own. Besides, what would we do with Antonia? It can't be so hard to find a babysitter for a few hours, she said, and clapped her hands to indicate I should get down to it right away. I can't wait for you to meet Horacio, he's such a great person. Something tells me you'll like him a lot. I smiled, filled with foreboding. Lately Laura often hinted that, while she was making changes to her life, I had got stuck in a rut. No one has the right to give up, she would say, as if in the abstract, a universal rallying cry aimed unmistake-ably at me. Guillermo lectured me along the same lines. I took no notice, considering that neither of them was in any position to tell me how to behave. The babysitter problem proved unexpectedly easy to resolve. Magically easy, I should say. I was at the pastry shop and it was as if the assistant read my mind. With Antonia on my hip I was selecting some buns, and the plump, vaguely disagreeable one with ruddy cheeks said, out of the blue, while steadily filling my basket: I finish work at half past seven, after that I'm free. I shook my head, blushing, then promptly nodded, like a bad comedian. Oh no, oh yes. The girl saw my embarrassment and laughed moistly at what I'd thought. No, no, quickly knocking any fantasies on the head: To look after the baby, I mean. I'm Lucrecia, and she wrote her mobile number on a card with the shop's logo. We made arrangements for the following evening. Antonia accepted her without fuss, and the pleasure seemed mutual. Laura would have been upset if she'd seen it. The dinner party wasn't in the studio after all because a pipe had burst and everything was flooded, so we went to a local seafood place. My first sight of Horacio more than bore out my expectations. Fleshy, toothy, overstated and ginger. Pale-blue eyes and a high-pitched voice, which every now and then he attempted to camouflage by affecting a throaty growl. The guests were seated around two tables pulled together to make a T, Horacio sat at the vertex, two places away from Laura. I hung back a bit before going to say hello, Laura introduced us, Horacio shook my hand forcefully while seeking my eyes with his, at once challenging and subjugating me. I hoped Laura had saved me a place but she hadn't. Free-for-all, she said, making circles with her forefinger in the air. The only empty chair was at the foot of the T, opposite Horacio. I hesitated, but strangers' voices encouraged me, so I took it. Laura raised her arm and loudly said my name. Horacio, already rather merry, brandished his glass and demanded a round of applause for 'Laura's friend'. It sounded sarcastic to me. Our positions at the top and bottom of the table facilitated a play of caustic glances from which I was unable to extract myself the whole evening. From the start, he saw me as a competitor and I saw him as an enemy. Horacio waved his arms, horsed around, talked and acted like a wizard. He bullied everyone at the table, including the waiter, who went along with it for the sake of the tip. Horacio embarked on a blow-by-blow account of his meeting with Jodorowsky in Paris. A guy in a million, a visionary. His voice reached me in snatches, I caught some words and missed others, depending on the emphasis, but as far as I could make out he was present at the moment when an afflicted boy broke through his autism with a shout (Leave me alone!), after those who were with him, Jodorowsky, the parents, a nurse and Horacio himself, had aped his behaviour for three days in a row. Magic, amazing! the man almost shrieked. As Laura gazed at him spellbound, I felt a mixture of jealousy and embarrassed pity. It's hard to explain, but for a moment I sensed that her inviting me to this gathering signified our farewell. A grand farewell in public. Even the food and drink were chosen by Horacio, the great interpreter of others' desire. Mussels, cod roe, whitebait and clams with Parmesan. The food was fine but rather greasy. Laura was eating with gusto and this too made her seem unfamiliar. I barely tasted what I was given, all the talk around me sounded empty or pretentious. At some point Horacio, flushed with wine, stood up behind the mountain of mussel shells which he'd just been using to make a funny mask, and left the table, looking literally about to explode. On an impulse I rose and went after him, not quite knowing what for. Laura shot me an inquisitorial look as if guessing my intentions, I gestured that I'd be right back, then dawdled a little to disguise my pursuit. At the door to the toilet I passed a tall blond man, clearly foreign, who stared at me with bright-eyed insistence. The basins were deserted. Horacio had placed himself in the middle of a row of three urinals, one hand splayed against the tiled wall for support, the other out of sight guiding the stream of piss. He was whistling. With no choice but to stand next to him, I unbuttoned my fly and mimed having a leak, though I didn't need one. Horacio lurched his head sideways, not recognising me at first, his stare penetrating, probing, abrasive. It exuded a sweet and malignant drug, with something sacred about it; here was the source of the spell he worked on the others, his congregation, his followers, and I was about to succumb. I looked away, at the puddled floor, the cisterns, anywhere, and mumbled like a fool: Nice place, isn't it? Horacio laughed noisily, spraying specks of food over the tiles, then went serious. He said: Laura's a doll . . . a bit out of your league, I'd have thought. I looked at him, flummoxed, mouth quivering, waiting for the jokey punchline. Instead Horacio goaded me with an animal grin as he shook off his meaty, treacherous penis. He zipped up and glanced at me again, moving his head negatively from side to side. Rooted to the spot, I concentrated on the whirling drain of the urinal. When I looked round, Horacio was standing a short way off with his back to me, in front of the wash-basin. I could see him through the mirror casually inhaling cocaine, using the nail of his little finger to smear it into both nostrils. It was while he was inspecting his teeth and gums, making atrocious sucking sounds, that I decided to kill him. His insult combined with the lack of witnesses convinced me that I had to do it, as much as if I'd planned it. I would have to be accurate, unhesitating, and avoid scuffles and commotion. Horacio had twice my brawn, though he was about six inches shorter, we could be grappling indefinitely. He would fight with his strength, I with my shame and honour. I cast about for something that would ensure a swift and certain death. For a moment I considered strangling him with my bare hands. Spotting a broken tile in a corner of the wall, I pulled on the edge and managed fairly easily to dislodge a piece that was broad at the base and sharp at the tip, a ceramic stalactite. A natural and perfect dagger. I was ready to plant it in his jugular without a thought for the gory spillage. I was enraged, all I wanted was to obliterate him. And I would have done it, I was seconds away, except that a youth with a beard suddenly burst in: Maestro!

Horacio smiled with open arms and patted his stomach. How could all these zealots worship such a cynic? I left the toilet clenched into a ball of hate. Back at the table, Laura avoided me, clearly not wanting to deal with my discomfort. She moved her jaws like a ventriloquist's dummy. She was probably doing cocaine as well, that would explain her erratic behaviour of late, her sudden mood shifts. It would explain everybody's egomania, starting with Horacio's, not to mention the way Marion was parading her addictions. The livelier the party grew, the more fed up I felt. I was cornered by a woman with a bad boob job and cigarette breath, bent on sharing what had happened to her on the way to the restaurant. I listened unwillingly, preserving a critical distance. She had been driving through the city centre when she was caught in a traffic jam. Stopped at the lights, she realised that she was split in two, her thoughts bombarded her with commands while her body was living in a prison. She mutinied: took her hands off the wheel, unclipped her safety belt and went on strike against reason . . . The last thing she remembered was a man in uniform knocking on the car window. She regained consciousness twenty minutes later, at the counter of a pizza house. Eyeballing me with ostentatious sexual intent, the woman rounded off her tale with a quote from the master: The power of the mind was invented by softies! Horacio, galvanised by booze, handed out pieces of paper on which everyone had to write 'an unconfessable desire'. Something really dark, he said in his gruffest voice. The papers were to be folded and put into the bread basket, and he would guess the author of each desire. Laura, who was still keeping well away, so that I only heard the high notes of her laughter, seemed thoroughly turned on by this idea. I waited for the biro to come round and wrote in capitals, without stopping to think: I'M GOING TO KILL YOU YOU BASTARD. I folded the paper four times, dropped it in the basket and, not so much from cowardice as driven by discomfort and irritation, excused myself with a wave to the nearest people and made for the exit. I took deep breaths of the swirling, storm-laden air. Laura had only invited me along to humiliate me, that much was clear, and I couldn't let her do it. I glanced back over my shoulder in time to see Horacio, blindfolded and coiffed with a turban, rustling through the bread basket about to pick up the first paper. It was too much, I took off just as the thunder started. The terrible nature of my gift came home to me: I would never be able to kill anybody outright. I tortured myself with thoughts of fate, my role in history, the place assigned to me in the pantheon of mediocrity, suspended on a high wire between the man I had become and the man I would have liked to be. I trudged for hours under a steady downpour until it got very cold. When I opened the door of the house in a far from decent state, laid to waste by the rain and my internal collapse, Lucrecia's eyes looked into mine from another world. I couldn't believe it. This was definitely not the same girl I'd left in charge of Antonia a few hours before. And yet it was, she was the same. Such a body she had, such loveliness . . . Lucrecia brought me a towel from the bathroom and it was a bit like I was her and she was me. I dried myself without moving, paralysed and happy. Shall I make you some tea? Or how about a shot of whisky? I said the car had died on me. She smiled, divining the lie. The transformation was so astounding, it simply could not be a trick of perception. She told me that Antonia had gone to sleep like an angel and only woken up once, clutching on to Lucrecia's finger. We drank camomile tea, whisky, and camomile with whisky. Instead of getting ready to go home, Lucrecia stayed and we talked. She didn't ask after Laura, she probably assumed we'd had a fight. We talked forever, one topic linking to the next, studying to the advent of spring, her siblings to my hobbies, the neighbourhood to life itself. Lucrecia insisted I call her Moomie, *all my friends call me that*, she thought her real name sounded harsh. She'd had enough of working at the pastry shop, it took up too much time and made her gloomy: It's a downer. She dreamed of doing something connected with nature, but didn't know exactly what. She stood up, walked towards me, and past me to the bookcase. What a lot of books! she exclaimed. I'm very fond of reading, I said, and added something I regretted at once, to do with muses and poets. Just kidding, I said hastily, and she confessed she had no sense of humour. As it was still pouring down outside I wondered whether to suggest she stay the night, but didn't dare, Laura might turn up at any minute. Well, I'll be going, she said, I wanted to keep her but couldn't find adequate reasons. Our conversation, her new presence, had made me forget I had to pay her. It was hard to settle the number of hours; she had stayed with me of her own accord, but I didn't want to take advantage. I ended up giving her twice the right amount, explaining it was on account, so she wouldn't refuse. For the future, I said. At the door I offered an umbrella which she parried with both hands like something preposterous, declaring:

Nobody uses umbrellas any more. Then, as we said goodbye, an unexpected thing occurred that acted on me like a drug. Lucrecia stretched up to give me a kiss on the cheek which landed, thanks to a prodigiously lucky miscalculation, almost full on my mouth. I couldn't get to sleep after that. How could I! There's nothing more delicious than the insomnia induced by new love. I made the most of this rapture by finishing *Resurrection*. Towards the end the hero seeks solace in the Sermon on the Mount, subscribing almost ecstatically to its moral precepts, convinced that were these to be implemented, as he thinks they easily could be, a new and essential society would spring up. He lies on a sofa, reflecting that 'we imagine ourselves to be masters of our lives, and that life is given us for enjoyment . . . This is a foolish belief. We were sent here by someone's will and for some reason.' I once heard or read somewhere that any good novel must contain at least one memorable scene. *Resurrection* is not a factory churning out the sort of iconic scenes that were Tolstoy's speciality; here the memorable aspect is the dream of reconstruction, a remaking of both the individual and the community. Laura gave her first sign of life at around seven in the morning. She sent a terse, curt text: Caught by the rain, stayed downtown. Her choice of a mute form of communication raised the stakes to a level from which it wouldn't be easy to back down. After pondering a range of responses I decided on indifference. I didn't want to appear weak and at the same time I'd let my anger show. Downtown? What did that mean? A hotel, someone's pad, Horacio's studio? The desire to do away with that brute was still there. I didn't dwell on it, instead the allusion to the storm made me recap my long hike, positively a feat, my arrival home, the magical encounter with Lucrecia, her kiss against the corner of my mouth. All my thoughts converged on her, I only had to shut my eyes to see her, hear her, smell her, almost touch her. I sat up, the book fell open in the middle and I read a line by chance: *How delightful, how delightful, oh, God, how delightful.* The screech of the bakery's metal shutters set off a vibration in me that I hadn't felt since I was thirteen. I waited for Antonia to wake up with my hands clasped over my navel. The brightness outside was projected onto the walls of the room, percolating through the slits of the blind in a mute, conceptual show. The emergence of love is always unforeseen. What does age matter, after all? What does it matter who the other person is? A baker, a hermit or a soap star. What counts is what she meant to me already, a swing of the helm in the arc of my life. Antonia awoke with a delicate whimper. I sprang as if catapulted out of bed, we gazed into each other's eyes, hers still crumpled, I hoisted her up and she hugged me with wise sweetness. That was it! She had powers too. Though inherited from me, hers were the opposite, they were powers of healing, she had no need to do harm in order to effect rebirth in others. Her innocence and my frustration explained why one gift was pure and the other depraved. Antonia was responsible for Lucrecia's wondrous metamorphosis, I didn't need more evidence. I kissed her over and over in gratitude for what she had wrought. She let herself be changed and dressed in one fluid sequence, it was past nine o'clock, I tucked her into the buggy with a bottle of milk. Outside the gate a tingle went through me that turned icy on entering the shop. Lucrecia was not behind the counter. I asked, and the harried cashier mumbled that she thought she'd resigned. I asked her to check, but she was already busy with another customer. Sick at heart, head hanging, I went out again. In front of the gate Antonia threw a tantrum. She kicked her legs furiously, which was unusual in her. Clearly not ready for home, she stuck out an arm and pointed into the distance, waving aimlessly. She wanted to go onwards.

My disappointment made me favour a getaway. Until now our morning outings had consisted of mandatory errands to the grocer's or the fruit and veg shop, or to pay a bill, and included a halt in the square on the way or the way back. I had not been much inclined to take walks for their own sake, and here she was rebuking me for it with a show of temper. It seemed a good opportunity to separate one thing from the other, fun from obligation. Two rituals carried out in the same motion end up being neither this nor that. The square had become a bland, humdrum destination, I would seek new horizons. And so it was that I discovered the municipal nature reserve, round the back of our block, between the parish church and the cemetery. Whoever had planned the town had obviously decided to concentrate everything in one place. It was two years since our move, and I'd never known about this wilderness behind us. Forever in the middle of renovation, due to the indolence of an endless succession of concrete-junkie bureaucrats, the reserve only survived thanks to the efforts of volunteers who met there every day, trusting in the promise of imminent regeneration. We ventured along a lush path beside a brook, until the buggy's wheels got bogged down. The landscape was evenly split between greenery and litter. At the exit we were stopped by a girl in dungarees with limpid eyes and hair like a broom. We're looking for volunteers, she said. Out of conscience or desperation, I'm not sure which, I agreed to help out. The basic task was to collect bottles, plastic and other detritus brought in by the river at high tide. Having to bend down over and over, sink my feet into the mud, breathe that half-natural, half-nauseating smell, swept my negative thoughts away. Nothing beats physical tiredness for reclaiming the pieces of one's being. Antonia joined in enthusiastically, and if at first I tried to prevent her getting dirty, I soon understood that she was responding to an ancestral call. While my job called for efficiency, bagging as many bottles as possible per minute, Antonia tended to postpone the recycling aspect in favour of contemplation: a small lid, a truncated tube or the wheel off a toy tractor would engross her until they had exhausted their potential, both practical and symbolic. We spent a busy couple of hours before being convened to the gallery of the former horticultural college, a majestic building ruined by neglect. We shared the meal in a circle. All was silence and harmony. After lunch they took us to see the Waste Museum, a display of refuse classified according to size, material and shape. We promised to return soon and continue the work. Completely exhausted, with aching back and damp clothes, I only remembered Lucrecia when I saw the bakery awning. I looked in, she wasn't there. I texted her: Did you get home OK? No reply. An hour later I tried again: Thanks for the chat! I felt like an idiot after the second text, she still didn't answer. In the evening I called her mobile and heard the digital voice droning that the number I had reached was not in service. That week I skipped my appointment with Guillermo for the first time, I hadn't the strength for the pressure of our encounters. Laura's absence lasted for several days. Rarely enquiring about Antonia, she claimed that work was keeping her till late and that was why she stayed in the city. She did text me some of the latest mottos: Jealousy is for the weak and loveless! Living in the mind is slavery! Freedom is an accursed and holy word! In other circumstances I would have protested against this behaviour, but in a way it was a relief not to see her. I never mentioned Horacio; by this stage I was not much put out by the possibility of her cheating on me. One morning as I was heading for the reserve, Guillermo intercepted me at the corner. We had never seen each other in the outside world or in sunlight. He braked by the kerb and lowered the polarised window. I was expecting you, he grunted from inside the car, without showing his face or acknowledging Antonia in her buggy, who kept straining forward as if to hear our exchange. I was busy . . . I said with an absurd twinge of guilt. Guillermo's response was to reseal himself inside his capsule, and the white Kia accelerated out of sight. Deprived of both Laura and Lucrecia, I vowed to devote myself entirely to the reserve and to being a father. It was hard to spend any length of time at home, I was haunted by memories, mechanically replaying the quarrels with one, the kiss of the other, the blood and dreams and soil in-between, all mixed up together within a gossamer web. The routine of community work centred me. I embarked on more substantial jobs, promoted from bottle collector to restorer of bridges and gangways. Antonia seemed happy in the new surroundings. Her native independence flourished in that quasi-wilderness. I lost sight of her for hours on end as she toddled or crawled down paths of her own making, largely outside the standard circuit. Just once, while varnishing a staircase banister, I felt a prick of unease. Quietly, not letting on to the others, I set off to track her through the weeds and scrub. A sure sign that it was she who magnetised me towards her is the fact that, with no knowledge of their destination, my footsteps did not err. I found her squatting in a thicket too dense for an adult like myself to penetrate. Antonia, I hissed a couple of times but she didn't respond, her attention focused on the ground between her legs. I fought my way closer on hands and knees, branches whipping my cheeks, on the verge of bafflement. When I finally made it to her side Antonia welcomed me with a pleased smile, she hadn't summoned me for nothing. She dropped her head, to make me do the same. In the midst of the dead leaves there was a hole about five centimetres wide. A hole, an aleph, an oracle. It would be easy to yield yet again to chaotic enumeration, as easy as it would be inadequate, let's just say that what I saw there had all the compelling force and clarity of the first tornado. I returned to my post feeling doubly stunned, the visions I'd seen and the powers possessed by my daughter were perfectly commensurate. Antonia continued to wander off, and I didn't like to interfere in her adventures. One afternoon, up on the main platform, I noticed a figure with its back to me that looked familiar. Tousled hair, small head, square shoulders forming a singular trapezium. Lucrecia? During the split second it took for me to straighten up and her to turn around, a thousand specious thoughts went through my mind. I realised I still adored her. A life with her was possible, things would sort themselves out as they always do, by dint of habit and of love. She looked more grown-up, seasoned, fuller, a third version of herself. Time recovered its normal speed and, stepping forwards, it hit me that she was pregnant, and by more than a few months. We said hello without mentioning the belly. She told me that she'd left the pastry shop in order to devote herself wholly to nature, and it was our talk that had encouraged her to take the plunge. The misunderstandings were mounting inside me when a curly-haired youth who looked vaguely like my past self but with a hooked nose, a stalwart among the volunteers, came up from behind and wrapped his arms round Lucrecia's shoulders. We introduced ourselves: José, José. Snap, he said, raising a hand for me to high-five. I asked some polite questions and they deluged me with information about their plans, a prospective trip, what they could look forward to, the little house on the island they'd just started to build: It's all going to be different now! I stopped listening. We said bye for now, I pulled off my gloves and knew I wouldn't see them again. As I retreated I was sure I had played a part in their union, indeed in some sense provoked it. Perhaps life was telling me something. That night, back home after a week away, Laura took my hands and asked me to look into her eyes: Do you love me? Thrown by the question, I shot back point-blank: Of course I love you! We hadn't exchanged a word for days, let alone of that sort. The bond between us had been reduced to a meticulous dramatisation of disaffection. And yet we were still a couple. Laura marked a pause before firing more darts: Would you do anything for my sake? If it's good for you ... Without judging me? Sit down, she ordered, I have something of vital importance to discuss. I suspected, correctly, that this something was related to the Wednesday sessions. Laura was on a roll, declaiming at me like an orator before an audience. We had avoided the subject of Horacio ever since that night in the restaurant; I swallowed my pride and decided to pay attention. In one of their last exercises, the protagonist had been Laura. She had talked about us, our squabbles and her issues with maternity, until eventually the story of her parents came up. According to her mother the encounter with her father had been a one-night stand, they'd never set eyes on each other again. They had met in a seedy bar where Nelson, that was her father's name, was performing, a tango singer who worked the coast in summer.

They spoke briefly on the phone when her mother was five months pregnant, and again shortly after Laura was born. Nelson agreed to send a little money, but never showed any interest in meeting his daughter. On her fifteenth birthday, Laura learned that her father had died a few weeks previously. Horacio proposed a role play to get to the bottom of the original trauma. Laura guided two companions in acting out the scene: Marion, playing the mother, accosted the supposed father, a bald chap who was apparently my neighbour at the Friendship Day supper but I couldn't for the life of me remember, they danced, they kissed, and wound up making love on the floor. Metaphorically, Laura specified, though they had entered so wholeheartedly into their roles that they began to strip off and very nearly fucked in earnest. After witnessing her own conception, Laura curled into a ball between Marion's legs and was 'delivered' into the hands of her father. The scene ended with the three of them hugging and saying they loved each other. Family was no longer an impossibility. The experience did Laura a power of good, she came out feeling freer and lighter. So much so that she wanted to celebrate her rebirth and, on Horacio's suggestion, went for a beer with some of the others. She ended up getting blind drunk like a teenager. The ensuing night was crystal clear in her memory, spent vomiting into the toilet bowl and then unable to sleep a wink. The next morning was dreadful, on top of the hangover she realised she'd made a fool of herself and, worst of all, that she was still carrying the burden of her abandonment. Over the following days the effects of the cure became detrimental. Laura was taciturn and depressed, with no energy for work, while her difficulties in relating to Antonia grew more acute. She hardly ate. Defeated by this evidence of relapse, she confided in Horacio who told her that her case was likely to be one of peculiar intricacy, with multiple causes, in which the perception of orphanhood was combined with a cult of the father figure arrested at the idolatry level. A knotty Oedipus complex that would be a challenge to sort out. According to Horacio, Antonia is really Antonio, the boy I wasn't, Laura explained with euphoric anguish. Had she been born a boy, her father would have taken notice of her. That rejection, which she now unconsciously reproduced by shunning her child as an image of her own fate, had turned her into a permanently vindictive person. At this point I was on the verge of interrupting: Antonia's situation was obviously quite distinct from hers, witness my presence in the home, almost like a mother's. Laura sat down before me, composing herself. Horacio says I have to sleep with my father and show him what I can do, he says I'm not my mother and that I too can take my pleasure and leave it, and that the only way to break my destructive patterns is to recognise my own plenitude. I want to be able to look at my daughter with loving eyes and not blame her for being a girl! she cried, almost aphonic. And in a final breathy squeak: I need you to help me! Laura gazed at me like a young virgin, she was in character already. Via a number of digressions, she outlined the task devised by Horacio with a view to extirpating the seed of her frustration. The plant itself remains the same, she said, making air quotes. Shaking the leaves creates a noise but to no effect, he who aspires to freedom must gird himself to plough the earth, chop from the root, submit to a transplant if need be. She was obviously parroting what she'd heard. Metaphors aside, the mission consisted in a consummation of incest, ideally on top of the father's grave. Once the latter had been dismissed as impracticable, given that Nelson, as far as Laura knew, had been cremated, I expressed consent. This was an emergency. All right, I said, we'll try. Laura relaxed at last and put her arms around me, and when she stepped back it was as if she was also taking a distance from the situation, her request, and all that had been said: At the end of the day, she sighed, life is a great big stage . . . And you almost never get to choose which character you play. I thought of the many doubts that had lately been revived in me by reading Tolstoy. The individual as the product of his environment was an outmoded idea, a catchphrase with no flesh on its bones. Politics are one thing, the emotions are something else. With the preamble over and the cultural discussion skirted, Laura brought me a picture of her father to look at. It was an amateur snapshot with the typical, yellow-tinted spontaneity of the seventies. The pose informal, a guitar carelessly slung across the thigh with the strings against the abdomen, one elbow propped in the hollow of the instrument, a cigarette pinched between thumb and forefinger in front of the mouth, the face wreathed in smoke. There was no need for particulars, I understood what she wanted from me. We settled on Friday night for our staging of the scene, once Antonia had gone to sleep. I'd only ever owned one suit in my life; I wore it to a series of fifteenth-birthday parties, later, duly altered, it had done for the odd wedding and for job interviews. When I went to fetch it from the wardrobe, I'd forgotten that on the last occasion I wore it I looked so ludicrous in the mirror that I had decided to give it to charity. Next day I went back to Guillermo's and was welcomed without admonishment. I thought of asking to borrow a suit but couldn't see how to explain, it would be better to simply help myself. I sped up the customary ritual, a bit of jazz, a few drinks, and a classic murder: a good dose of rat poison dissolved in a small glass of liqueur. I entered his bedroom and selected a sober, grey, double-breasted affair. As I went downstairs a momentary qualm assailed me. Killing for killing's sake is one thing, killing and stealing isn't really the same. Friday came and with every hour that passed my enthusiasm and excitement grew. I mounted a veritable mise en scène. The house was turned into a tavern, my prejudices fell away, I realised that I too could benefit from the experiment. I bought candles, olives, cheese and two bottles of expensive wine. Slotting the photo of Laura's father into the frame of the bathroom mirror, I recreated the character with careful attention to detail. My features were a long way from his, it would have taken surgery or a latex mask, but the suit, the buttonhole and the gel slicking my hair flat made for a fair approximation. I also shaved off my beard, something I hadn't done since the first cold spells. I was not perhaps the spit of Laura's father, but I definitely wasn't myself, either. Pausing, angling the scissors to tidy up my sideburns, I was struck by how many new trades I'd learned as a result of being unemployed: housewife, gardener, killer, cook and now actor, practically overnight. Pro bono in every case. They say that money ultimately destroys the most deep-seated vocation. When Laura arrived, no doubt still preoccupied by office business, she fell straight into the maw of the absurd. At the sight of me in costume, with the guitar nearby and the table lit by candles, she stifled her hilarity by clapping both hands over her mouth and diving into the bathroom. She had forgotten all about the date with her dad. She kept apologising through the door, crying or laughing, I couldn't tell. I downed two glasses of wine and lit a cigarette. I hadn't smoked for years but dug out a packet I'd seen lying in a drawer, the situation certainly merited a puff or two. What will be, will be. Laura emerged from the bathroom five minutes later with rouged lips and eyes outlined in black, her hair self-consciously rumpled. With no more ado we gave ourselves over to the play. I put on a Troilo record and we began chatting with the awkwardness of any first meeting. Contrary to what you would expect, given the practice she'd had at the sessions and my inexperience, she plainly found it harder to get into character than I did. Admittedly her part was a more demanding one: I was Nelson, tango crooner and nomad, while she went on being Laura. We talked about music, the changing times, I praised her eyes and her luminous smile. When I reached for her hand, gently and wholeheartedly, I gathered we were doomed to fail. Laura's shoulders quivered and though she did not exactly recoil, I felt her fingers contract. I tried to press on by strok- ing her knee but she jerked back, got up and shut herself in the bedroom, excusing herself: I'm sorry, I can't! This is so ridiculous, it's making me worse! And she burst out crying, stamping her foot and throwing things on the floor, repeating: I'm so stupid! My life is shit! Laura's screams and moans plunged me into a similar distress. We tried twice more, and at the third attempt we managed some kissing and tentative groping. Laura broke down again, but I was highly aroused and the evidence was more extended than usual. I lifted her skirt, nudged her panties aside and pushed my cock into her there and then, on top of the kitchen table. I felt more of a Nelson than ever, slightly brutal, but effective. Laura gradually loosened up, I knew it by her groans and the way she clutched my buttocks, until she said, shyly at first and then with wild abandon: Fuck me, Daddy! Harder! I love you! And I went: Laura, Laura baby, you're amazing . . . How big you've grown! We had sex for hours, unbridled sex on the far side of the senses. Next morning Laura disappeared. Absent once more, she would phone in the middle of the night and leave strange messages amid sobbing and raving, as if speaking in a foreign language. Instead of getting better, she continued to plummet even when it seemed she'd hit rock bottom. Thursday of that week I went to Guillermo's and dispatched him more viciously than ever. I soaked him in alcohol from the waist down and set him alight to a string-led version of 'Petite Fleur'. I stood and watched for some time. Guillermo was reeling to a curious cadence, grim and comical at once, a sublimation of violence and death into art and motion. Burning Guillermo marked the climax of my homicidal urge. Returning home with glowing cheeks, it struck me how everything that mattered in my life took place on a Thursday. I pictured the week like a mountainside, which it took me seven days to ascend and descend. The final approach to the summit began on Wednesday evenings, when Laura came home after her workshop and I never knew what I'd be in for. A long and unquiet night would await me. On Thursdays I'd start out with altitude sickness and even so, despite the tiredness, would spring into a super-active mode. By evening, just steps from the crater, my accumulated energy would be straining towards destruction. It had been like that from the start, but I'd only just worked it out. During the final ritual, dancing on the edge, the rule was to improvise as freely as possible. I didn't always succeed, of course. The worst part came after the crime had been committed. A sickening headlong descent, a crash that lasted no time at all, while recovery could take days. Back on level ground, at the foot of the mountain, came the time of reconstruction: inventory of limbs, reacquaintance with every part of oneself, rescue of the soul from blackness. Reaching the summit is a materialistic goal, peace is attained earlier, in contemplation, along the way. It's as simple as anything, but it's true. On Thursdays I indulged myself completely, and I also gave myself completely. Narcissism and detachment overlapped on that edge. Thursday belongs to Jupiter, and Jupiter regulates light and darkness across the universe in aid of its craving for drama. The relationship with Guillermo ended abruptly. There was no decline, corollary or epiphany, our last meeting was as trite as it was predictable. In a flash the mental snapshots I had of him collapsed one on top of the other, like a domino chain of human features. Any change of cycle, and this would be a textbook example, is triggered by a number of simultaneous signs. Because on that very afternoon, when she got home from work, Laura achieved her own catharsis. The moment I saw her coming down the hall, a strange pang of fear and pity went through me. Her face was a jigsaw puzzle full of gaps. Fortunately Antonia was having her afternoon nap, she did not witness her mother's bawling or her despair. I was preparing the ground for grass seeds, in the unconfident hope of treading on a lawn come summer. It was less a gardening activity than an inner struggle, a wistful desire to cloak aridity in life. The spade that had stood for months in the pile of earth behind me symbolised my paralysis, and also my basest instincts. And if I didn't have the courage to shoulder that burden, I could always dodge the issue, masking the inexorability of fate with concrete, positive actions. Recently I'd seen a harrowing film on television, replete with murder, incest and rape, whose plot unfolded backwards to the hero's birth. The film's moral was simplistic and Manichean, its final image, a baby crawling on bright green grass, was designed to convey hope and dire warning at once; I enjoyed it all the same, and the ending had, in fact, inspired me to embark on this new project. Over and above allegory, a lawn increases your chances of well-being. Laura was haggard and silent, a phantom projection of herself. Huddled in a corner of the garden, she gave me no time to say hello but dissolved into tears like a woebegone virgin. I thought about myself and all my failings. It was a dammed-up grief, suddenly decompressed. I wanted to hush her, but stopped myself and let her vent at leisure. After a few minutes Laura calmed down and only then, crushed as she was, resorted to words. She stammered: They made me feel like total scum. She had left the group, or they had expelled her, depending how you looked at it. I hugged her and lent an ear right there, under the lemon tree. She'd had a heated argument with Horacio, and Marion had sided with the maestro: Can you believe it? My friend! According to Laura they had gone overboard, made mincemeat of her. She didn't go into the details, nor did I ask for them. It was horrible, they're sick, she said. The tears ran down her cheeks and fell on my shoulder or straight to the ground. By a serendipitous trick of the light, half her face was in shadow while the other half was on fire in the slanted rays of the setting sun. The contrasts were shifting and mercurial, black moths fluttering just over her cheekbones. I listened attentively, still holding the rake in the midst of the overturned clods. Deep down he's a sadist! A massive bastard! No different to the rest of them, they're all as bitter as hell. I felt a secret satisfaction. Laura had been poisoned by her own medicine; although Horacio had long ceased to obsess me, my contempt for him endured. The worst thing is feeling let down by a person I trusted so much. If Horacio is a snake, then the whole thing was a farce and the cure was pure fiction. I was tempted to annoy her by saying, What cure? but contained myself in time. All that stuff we did together, she went on emphatically, raising an eyebrow in what I took for acknowledgement of my diligence in recreating the father figure. The guy's a bluffer with no ideas of his own, if Jodorowsky only knew what he gets up to in his name . . . A different crying, purer and more urgent, put her off her stride. It came from Antonia, timely and somehow miraculous, gazing at us from the edge of the garden. Laura's face underwent a magical transformation, she let off a burst of convulsive laughter which a casual observer would have mistaken for derangement. Antonia had put her under one of her spells. With a startled look at me, Laura took a deep breath and threw her arms artlessly, unreservedly wide, I feared the worst; Antonia didn't move for a few frozen seconds, then ran towards her. I understood that she held our fate in her hands. All of a sudden we were a family, not perhaps a normal family, but still standing, at least. Laura and Antonia had a lot of catching up to do, that's why I didn't join in their embrace. The afternoon's events were to what happened later that night as the shoot is to the seed. After supper, the three of us eating together at last, I cleared the table, put the dishes to soak and said to Laura what I said every Thursday: I'm going to return the neighbour's spade. Like a mantra, not naming Guillermo; my initial, indeed my only, strategy had been the appearance of aloofness. There's a point at which scheming and habit become indistinguishable. That night, however, due to the emotional release of finally breaking through her zombie shell, Laura bridled at the set phrase instead of ignoring it and raised her voice: What spade? I was already turning the handle, one foot in the air, poised to cross over to the outside world. My dismay was patent but Laura persisted, drawing a virtual spade in the air. I looked at her and blushed, she came over, took my hands and kissed me on the forehead, a redemptive kiss. Go on then, give him his spade once and for all, she said, but don't come home too late, eh? I smiled lamely, I could have charged her with any number of offences considerably more improper than my sorties to Guillermo's, but kept quiet. I felt diminished. Laura's remark was the spur that made me pull out the spade and fill in the pit at long last. It took thirty-two spadefuls, four fewer than had originally been required to dig it. I mused on soil evaporation, ectoplasm and the number of grammes a dead soul is said to weigh. Before going upstairs to Guillermo's, in the spirit of reordering the direction of events, I took care to replace the spade where I had got it from that first night. Guillermo met me with his mobile to his ear, underlining my lateness with the standard gesture of tapping the wrist with the forefinger. He was in jeans, barefoot and bare-chested, plainly upset. I'd never seen him in such a state. He paced the room like a caged beast, making figures of eight, zigzagging or cutting diagonally across while squabbling on the phone with his mother or his sister. I could never tell which one it was, in both cases he rounded off his irate and escalating monologues with: You're driving me crazy! And whereas my arrival normally made him break off whatever he was doing to give me his attention, this time was different. Without ceasing to talk, he evicted me from the couch with a snap of his fingers and sent me to the kitchen for something to drink. Such tactlessness was him all over, an apparent compliment that puts the guest in the wrong for not feeling easy enough to make themselves at home. With a hunch that the coming hours would be crucial, I opted for the whisky bottle and poured two generous glasses on the rocks. Guillermo had started sweating heavily and did nothing to staunch the drops that covered his forehead, beaded his chest and dripped from his back onto the carpet. It wasn't that hot, he was stoked up by the argument. Moving past me he shook his head hard, as though to dismiss some unwelcome idea, and thoroughly spattered me. A yelp midway between pain and hysteria signalled the end of the conversation: They're driving me crazy! It was addressed to me, he had hung up, miming a wish to chuck the handset out the window. We toasted each other suggestively, or so it seemed to me in retrospect. I began to think you weren't coming, he huffed. I shrugged my shoulders, what would be the point of relaying the latest developments at home? He rolled his eyes apologetically, I smiled. He confessed to feeling nervous. Because of the trip, he said, it's so soon. What trip? What do you mean, what trip? I told you a hundred times, I'm off to Paris next week. A packed schedule of interviews, museum visits, meetings with designers, architects and interior decoration firms awaited him. He had lined up a programme in a million. We clinked glasses again: To Paris! But let's not get sidetracked, he said. There was still a major gap in my musical education: jazz fusion. Guillermo held forth on origins and precursors, and reviewed some exemplars of the genre. We drank, we listened to a dozen tracks or more, time ticked by and I couldn't wait for the moment when he'd play 'Petite Fleur', I felt a real longing to get back to Laura. Instead matters took an embarrassing, if not altogether unexpected, turn. Guillermo sat down beside me, took a long slug of whisky, smiled and said: I've been thinking . . . I'd love you to come with me. Crazy notion, I know! I was dumbstruck, not so much by what he'd said as by the way he moved his lips. He started talking about the trip, the itinerary encompassing five countries and a jazz festival, the cities we could visit, and in a distracted moment gave me the first kiss. His breath smelled impressively of citrus. Anticipating my discomfiture, Guillermo quickly grabbed the back of my head and kissed me again, with a frankly wet and open mouth, making free with his tongue. He slid closer and closer on the smooth leather couch, next thing I was enfolded in his arms. There was a pause and I experienced two successive and opposed reactions. From initial stupor, translated into a certain stiffening of the muscles, I moved on to finding these kisses very natural and, vanquishing bigotry, surrendered to the most human game of all. The truth is that kissing a man felt much like kissing a woman, and elicited a passionate response. All the same, when Guillermo unbuttoned my shirt to stroke my nipples I fell straight back into the cultural spiderweb. Apparently untroubled by my bashfulness, he poured himself another scotch and squeezed my hand. I want you to come with me, he repeated, I'm serious. It's a once-in-a-lifetime opportunity! He looked into my eyes. I know we'd have a great time together. We fancy each other and we have great chats, what else is there? I swallowed and said: Thanks, but no. I invoked Laura and Antonia, the rough patch we'd been going through. Guillermo stood up twitchily and began to berate me, as if I was his mother or his sister. Calling me Mr Loser. Telling me that life was too good to bury oneself in a hole to avoid it. Wondering if I planned to spend the rest of my days being a housewife.

Because everything about me was so pathetic . . . You'll be growing a cunt and a pair of tits soon! Clearly offended by my refusal, Guillermo made increasingly spiteful taunts which fell so flat that they appeased rather than angered me. It was his vexation talking. Seen from the outside, I had more cause that night than ever before to wipe him off the map, yet there was nothing inside me that pushed me to do it. In the absence of alienation, crime becomes impossible. Guillermo hadn't lied. Spying through the window, I observed the very moment the minicab came for him. I watched him lock the front door, put his bags in the boot and climb into the car. We didn't say goodbye, the better to spare him a further instalment of our black and sentimental comedy. As soon as the vehicle pulled away, I vowed to renounce my strange skill for ever. The following Thursday when I rang the bell purely out of habit, an incisive female voice confirmed that Guille was away. It was the first time I'd ever heard a voice through that intercom, and the first time I'd heard him called by his pet name. Could I have given up everything to run away with him? Definitely not. On the other hand, one wasn't treated to that kind of invitation every day. To see Paris, London, the Coliseum in Rome. When would such an opportunity present itself again? But there was no time for regrets, as a few days later Laura, whose relationship with Antonia was back on a reasonable footing, came up with a proposal: Let's get away for a bit, we've earned it. Her mother had written to say that she was going to cross the pond from Uruguay. We organised our journey at full speed. Laura's mother arrived by ferry on Thursday night, Friday morning we embarked. During our few hours together I wondered if I reminded her of Nelson, I didn't dress like him but I had adopted the sideburns and the hairstyle, minus the gel, but swept back. It must have stirred some recollection or other, if so she gave no hint of it. Antonia saw us off without a peep, and I did worry whether we were doing the right thing, leaving her in the hands of a grandmother who was a virtual stranger to her. I reassured myself with the thought that she had after all brought up Laura, a fairly normal person. On the ferry, not long after we set sail, an androgynous-looking youth sat down opposite us. Do you mind? he said after he'd made himself comfortable. It was a plum spot by the big forward window, four small armchairs around a low table. His intrusion bothered me. There were plenty of free seats but he had chosen to sit right there. What time is it? Laura asked me in a low voice. Five to ten, the young man answered promptly, cocking the screen of his phone at us and segueing into the unpunctuality of the service: As it's a monopoly, nobody gives a toss. I take it three or four times a month, he went on, you'd think they were carrying cod instead of people. The crew's a bunch of primates. This rant had been set off by a question that wasn't even directed at him. Over the course of the journey we discovered that that was how he worked: a single word unleashed a spate of other words, an unstoppable torrent of triteness. Laura nodded politely and made the mistake of comparing the river service with the railways. Fixing us with his protuberant eyes, the interloper was off again: The trade union mafia and the manipulation of the workers are blatant proof of . . . I jumped up, saying I'd get some coffees. When I returned, it can't have been more than seven or eight minutes later, the fellow was going on about the havoc wreaked by European colonialism in the mines of Potosí. I had been given the power to dispatch bores like him without remorse. I made a mighty effort to withstand the temptation, and we lost him when we went through immigration. The rest of the journey to Montevideo was by coach, we sat in silence, Laura on the window side and me by the aisle. We dozed, head leaning against head. At the bus terminal we took a taxi to the hotel, an old building in the historic part of town that had been refurbished on the hoof. We spent three incomparable days together, very close to the ideal of love. We feasted, got drunk, danced for blocks and blocks behind a group of *candombe* drummers, lay face-up on the beach under the stars. We made love a lot, and split our sides laughing. At our neuroses, at Jodorowsky's maxims, at my Nelson get-up, at Antonia's temper, at Laura's benders, at a couple of skaters who kept popping up everywhere. There was time for reflection as well. Laura recapped her involvement with Horacio and the therapy group. She had got over her anger, and affirmed that the experience had shown her things about herself that otherwise would never have come to light. No pain, no gain, a pet phrase of Horacio's which she left floating in the air. The healing process in the aftermath of those earthquake days had wrought major changes in her. As if she'd dropped her personality mask, she said. I too had gone through big changes: losing my job, the upshot of that experience, the role reversal. I opened up as much as I could. I spoke about the future, my anguish in the face of uncertainty, my youthful dreams. I didn't feel like starting again, I had managed to carve out a place for myself at home, largely thanks to Antonia's good offices. Laura grew tearful, something inside her wasn't mended yet. I didn't mention Guillermo, of course, although in some veiled way I named him. On the last day we visited the funfair by the river. We rode the Ferris wheel and bumper cars and more, then sauntered gaily down the boulevard with a bottle of beer. It was as we drew level with the lighthouse, I believe, that Laura began to talk about my neglected talents, my facility with words, the passionate letters I wrote her when we were courting, those wild New Year messages I used to send out: the potential for a book. I could get people to read you just like that, she said, clicking her fingers. I laughed dismissively, gulped the last of the beer and fastened my gaze on the horizon, maintaining a forbidding silence. Because in paying me such compliments she was also pouring salt on the wound. As we walked on, the sun melting into the river like a crimson pudding, something became clearer. If you can't think of anything, start with yourself. Or do you mean to say nothing's happened to you this past year? Laura didn't know the half of it, yet she'd hit the nail on the head. I couldn't waste any more time! We reached the Montevideo terminal at nightfall. Laura was worn out, with a migraine that kept making her clutch her head, the whole thing had been too intense. I, on the other hand, was excited. As soon as we'd left the city behind, Laura took a painkiller and fell asleep. Did I have a story to tell? Most certainly. But I didn't want to write for the sake of writing. My book would aim to be a rigorous, definitive document. It had to reflect a real phenomenon, fantastic but real. Truly real. A crucial element was missing here. I needed evidence of the prodigy, I had to understand the logic. The devil's in the detail, that's the thing, that's the great lacuna of the Gospels, the ellipsis that bolsters the agnostics' incredulity. Whenever I try to puzzle out how Guillermo could recover from his injuries and burns, how the gashes I made healed up, how the damaged organs repaired themselves, Christ or the pigeon come to mind. Neither is of any use, I have to see before I can believe. My imagination has always been poor, a sterile field in which the smallest green shoot is quick to denounce itself as deception, as artifice. Literature is so vain! Thus it was that while Laura slept with her head on my shoulder and the Uruguayan countryside undulated past beyond the verges, I pondered the ingredients of a writing fit for the future. Useful and positive. Our homecoming was anything but easy. Laura and I were living an idyll, the trip had brought us closer than ever before, our relationship had reached heights to which not long ago we didn't think we could aspire. Being in love is always a wonder, but to touch that peak again at the end of a dogged climb up the slippery scree, that's true love. A far cry from our footloose jaunt, so light of baggage, at the beginning of it all. This state of grace we had reconquered, when no one would have thought it possible any more, smacked of the chimerical. And now what? Antonia greeted us with a hissy fit, Laura's mother wafted ghost-like through our lives. The day Laura returned to work, she found out she'd been reinstated in her old job. She was ecstatic as she gave me the news, we toasted with champagne as if we were still on the road. You know what this means, don't you? I raised my eyebrows, sincerely mystified. Don't you see? I'll be your editor, without intermediaries . . . There was no getting out of it. And while initially I let myself be dazzled by the vision of my book, as the night went on I found myself appalled at the insuperable nature of the task ahead. One thing was clear: in order to realise the project I would have to repeat the experiment one last time, document what took place and bear witness by gathering and presenting the evidence. I had of course forsworn the exercise of my gift, but now it pressed itself on me as a solution to the enigma, like a reflexive, final, exegesis. But who? Guillermo was thousands of miles away, who knew when he'd be back. Besides, our relationship had taken rather a knock when I snubbed him. I had to think of something else. Animals? That was a possibility, though it would lack the transcendental meaning I sought to impress on the affair. There were plenty of neighbours on our block, but I couldn't face having to cultivate a new acquaintance. Lucrecia was not a candidate, especially in her current condition. Horacio, though I no longer hated him, was worth considering. But I ruled him out as well, too loud to make a good victim. The answer came from Antonia, literally given by her hand. Like the mark of a paradoxical destiny. Mysticism is highly beneficial in everyday life, a stimulus like no other. Some tiny unfathomable nothing can clear our path to the epic dimension, spiritual or material. Such signs often, not to say always, issue from the least expected quarter. My strange gift plus the chance of a book called for a third leg that would endow these with meaning and balance. We in the West, believers and unbelievers alike, are partial to trinities. I am no exception, the outstanding traits of my personality and appearance residing precisely in their ordinariness. This, for all its mortifications, led me towards a kind of truth. With these drives working towards a single goal, though far from converging, one morning while I was preparing lunch something extraordinary happened. I was chopping onions on a wooden board when suddenly: *Remember the blaze in the fireworks factory?* It took me a moment to get that the voice was coming from the radio. I associate with that moment a stinging in my eyes, a welling up, followed by a small rush of shock. I stopped what I was doing and listened to the court report. The owner, his two sons, his son-in-law and the company lawyer had been charged with deliberately burning the place down to cash in on the insurance, with the collusion of a council inspector. The judge had sentenced them to custody without bail. I won't deny that the news filled me with gloating pleasure, celebrated with a smile at the kitchen window. The owners' attitude epitomised the pernicious dialectic that is branded onto the national character. Both immigrants and creoles harbour an anthropophagic streak that regularly prompts them to throw everything away on a bet, reinforcing their original dispossession. That loss was mother to a resentment that primes subsequent generations to re-enact the cannibalism in whatever form suits the time. A periodic summons to destruction and resurgence. Take a look at history, it's all there: rich men, lovers, artists, frittering away their works, the better to recognise themselves in downfall. The factory fire was unquestionably an instance of this tradition. The surprise turn taken by the case, as the reporter put it, left sacked workers in an advantageous position for suing the company, with a good chance of winning compensation. My initial glee gave way to an opposite emotion. I pictured a gaggle of lawyers and bureaucrats fighting for some illusory award. I was not prepared for such a thing. My ruminations were interrupted by a rumble of collapse behind me. I spun round, not understanding what I was seeing. A mountain of books at the foot of the shelves. Antonia was buried underneath, one of her legs sticking out of the pile, her small elbow peeping between spines and jackets. After a second's paralysis I strode forwards and rapidly relieved her of the weight, beginning with her head. Once she was completely freed, I reconstructed the accident. Her attempt to climb to the uppermost shelves had brought a whole row of books down on top of her. If she had been a different weight, if the bookshelf hadn't been screwed to the wall, it might have been fatal. I felt her head, her arms, her back, checking

for injuries, my stricken face at odds with her seren-
ity. Oblivious to the danger she'd been in, Antonia
was thrilled by the power of the experience. Desire
had lured her too far and she revelled in this, clearly.
I kissed her cheeks and forehead. Holding her tight
I felt an obstruction between her chest and mine. I
leaned back and saw, clutched in her left hand, a
thin, scuffed paperback with a flimsy cover which
I recognised at once: *The Death of Ivan Illich*. From my
days as a compulsive prowler of second-hand book-
shops. The coincidence shook me. Tolstoy, again!
This novel encompassed everything, my devotion
to the Russians, death and resurrection. But Antonia
had not finished with me yet. I sat her in her chair,
drew the book from her hand, meeting no resistance,
and began to leaf through it. Something slid from
between the pages and fell to the floor. I bent to
retrieve a photograph lying face down. It was of
Laura, that indelible picture I had taken of her standing in front of an antique hearse on our first trip
together. My euphoria turned to horror in the space
between an exhalation and an intake of breath. Was
this the answer to my search? I crouched on the
floor and stared at Antonia. Could a small girl really
be dictating such a plan? I shook my head hard and
slowly calmed myself, afraid of going crazy. My

offspring, a part of me projected into the future, was showing me the way. The mandate was transparent, my book had to be the story of Laura's resurrection. Antonia, or some higher energy manifest through her, had completed the sought-for trinity. My chest swelled at this discovery of the missing link. The circle was so perfect that it devolved into a labyrinth: to sublimate the beloved in her highest form and pierce the mystery. I confess it wasn't easy to take the next step, I needed several weeks to steel myself. During that period, among ups and downs, we managed to rub along rather well. Until one morning I awoke feeling firm in my decision. The scheme was simple and foolproof. I converted the bedroom into a home-movie set, concealing the camera behind the television; I even carried out focus and lighting tests, using myself as a stand-in. To break with the supremacy of Thursdays I scheduled the event for the last Friday in April, the first real night of autumn. Laura arrived home early. I made a *picada* of walnuts, sliced pork, hard cheese, capers and maraschino cherries. To drink, white wines, both sweet and dry. After supper, with Antonia fast asleep in her cot, Laura proposed a game of chess, like in the old days. It had been one of our favourite pastimes. We were neither of us good players or cunning strategists, in our world the winner was whoever didn't get distracted, which usually meant Laura. The great enjoyment was to watch the other's face in the throes of concentration. We liked to mount a little ritual around vodka and almonds. The endgames were frantic, we almost always wound up in bed. At one stage we became quite obsessive, turning without meaning to into collectors of boards and pieces. First came a set I'd inherited from my grandfather, a classic board of dark wood with ivory chessmen. Others followed, which we amassed like fetishes: stumbled upon by chance, at a street market, in a store window, in a junk shop or online. We got to own about a dozen, made of acrylic or cork, magnetic, travel-sized, featuring Indians v gauchos, hippies v yuppies, plus a marble one bought in Brazil. Our various relocations were prejudicial to this hobby; the most fragile sets fell by the wayside, as did those with the smallest or quirkiest pieces. In the end only my grandfather's, the basic, faithful set, survived. One Christmas Laura bought a floating set and we spent the whole of January in the pool, drinks to hand and sunglasses on, splashing each other whenever the match went against us. Those were happy times. It was life that put paid to our interest and practice. Restaging a perfect past, we played again that night. Laura was looking particularly lovely, each move she made like the promise of something else. The game unfolded evenly until almost the end, when I made a stupid play that left my queen exposed. Laura spotted it with a smile and reacted ruthlessly, two swift moves and she checkmated me. You let me win, she said in a reproachful voice. And it was so hard to argue against that, to insist on the thought-lessness of my action, that I found myself acquiescing to what was not the case. We kissed and looked in on Antonia among the glimmers and shadows of her dangling universe, together at the threshold of her room. Laura went for a shower and I lay on the bed reading. Looking up I glimpsed the jut of the camera draped in a hankie, it all seemed nonsense now. I no longer cared what might happen, the idea could remain a draft and that would be fine by me. Suddenly I turn my head and Laura is standing over me, naked and enlarged. She appeared taller, stronger, she had put her hair up and shaved her pubis. We kissed for a long time. Don't do anything, she whispered in my ear before undressing me. We made love very differently to when I was being Nelson, no need to pretend, every inch of our bodies was connected, we throbbed in unison. Laura had multiple orgasms. I only had one, at the end, in a different dimension. I was thus engaged, lying on top as in an old-fashioned married couple, male over female, when I opened my eyes and met hers, willing, wide and moist. That's when I remembered the plan, no longer a plan so much as an arcane summons from the beyond. It's a game, I informed her as I pulled the pillow from under her head and crushed it on her face. The movement was as smooth as the slide of the spade from between the bags of sand and quicklime the first time I killed Guillermo. Laura didn't protest, she let me, adjusting her body to my rigidity until she ran out of air. With a rapid reflex I pinned her wrists with my knees and her thighs with my feet to contain the juddering. I was her Adonis, her executioner. The resistance seemed to go on for ever, asphyxiation took place in stages, spasmodically, and required brute, shattering strength from me. It's hard to be specific but I could say, symbolically at least, that her last sigh coincided with my ejaculation. The small death and the great, conjoined in a single act. I put off removing the pillow, afraid of lacking fortitude for what I'd see. But to lose my nerve would have been worse; her face appeared frozen in bliss, set in the frightening beauty evoked by Tolstoy: 'Why had he suffered?

Why had he lived? Does he now understand?' I kissed her brow and proceeded thereafter like a professional. I got semi-dressed and hurried to switch on the camera. Reassured by the red light, I crossed the floor on my hands and knees, threw a last look round to make sure everything was in place and shut the door. An electric shock coursed through me, the stir of sex, death and adrenalin had propelled my being onto a heightened plane. I was obliged to lean against the wall so as not to lose my balance while I finished putting on my shoes, my legs would not stop shaking. I must have drunk a litre of water to slake the overwhelming thirst. Now that I go back over each step, I feel I've been as conscientious as I could. It's half past one, Antonia, I've just checked her, is asleep on her back with the gentle purr that saves me putting out a hand to make sure she's breathing. A tiny engine that fills me with pride and hope. Nothing bad can happen with her nearby. A long night lies ahead, and time must be killed somehow or other. I've made a thermos of coffee like I used to when I was a student. I always loved working through the small hours, alone or with others, prior to delivering an essay or sitting an exam. There was something mystical about it all, an unspoken belief that one belonged to a cell imbued with the ability to put the world to rights through the study of plankton, ancient philosophy or logarithms. Just like during my golden all-nighters of yore, I turn on the radio when I get sleepy. I tune into one of those nocturnal shows that play music from bygone decades on request, perfect company for loneliness or lassitude. Perhaps someone will think to request a version of 'Petite Fleur', well, that would be beyond coincidence. I myself used to call up and leave a message sometimes. I've always liked those programmes with a lot of music and few words.

Dear readers,

As well as relying on bookshop sales, And Other Stories relies on subscriptions from people like you for many of our books, whose stories other publishers often consider too risky to take on.

Our subscribers don't just make the books physically happen. They also help us approach booksellers, because we can demonstrate that our books already have readers and fans. And they give us the security to publish in line with our values, which are collaborative, imaginative and 'shamelessly literary'.

All of our subscribers:

- receive a first-edition copy of each of the books they subscribe to
- are thanked by name at the end of our subscriber-supported books
- receive little extras from us by way of thank you, for example: postcards created by our authors

BECOME A SUBSCRIBER, OR GIVE A SUBSCRIPTION TO A FRIEND

Visit andotherstories.org/subscribe to help make our books happen. You can subscribe to books we're in the process of making. To purchase books we have already published, we urge you to support your local or favourite bookshop and order directly from them – the often unsung heroes of publishing.

OTHER WAYS TO GET INVOLVED

If you'd like to know about upcoming events and reading groups (our foreign-language reading groups help us choose books to publish, for example) you can:

- join the mailing list at: andotherstories.org/join-us
- follow us on Twitter: @andothertweets
- join us on Facebook: facebook.com/AndOtherStoriesBooks
- follow our blog: andotherstoriespublishing.tumblr.com

Current & Upcoming Books

IOSI HAVILIO (b. 1974 Buenos Aires) became a cult author in Argentina after his debut novel *Open Door* was highly praised by the outspoken and influential writer Rodolfo Fogwill and by influential Argentine critic, Beatriz Sarlo. *Petite Fleur* is his fifth novel.

LORNA SCOTT FOX is a journalist, editor and translator who has lived all over the world. She has written for the *London Review of Books*, the *TLS* and the *Washington Post*, translated many books from French and Spanish, and edited Yuri Herrera's *Signs Preceding the End of the World*.